ALL BY MYSELF,
ALONE

MARY HIGGINS CLARK

ALL BY MYSELF, ALONE

SIMON &
SCHUSTER

London · New York · Sydney · Toronto · New Delhi

A CBS COMPANY

First published in the US by Simon & Schuster, Inc., 2017
First published in Great Britain by Simon & Schuster UK Ltd, 2017
A CBS COMPANY

A CIP catalogue record for this book is available from the British Library

Hardback ISBN: 978-1-4711-6281-7
Trade Paperback ISBN: 978-1-4711-6282-4
eBook ISBN: 978-1-4711-6283-1

This book is a work of fiction. Names, characters, places and incidents are either
a product of the author's imagination or are used fictitiously. Any resemblance
to actual people living or dead, events or locales is entirely coincidental.

Printed and bound by CPI Group (UK) Ltd, Croydon, CR0 4YY

Simon & Schuster UK Ltd are committed to sourcing paper that is made
from wood grown in sustainable forests and support the Forest Stewardship
Council, the leading international forest certification organisation. Our
books displaying the FSC logo are printed on FSC certified paper.

In memory of my mother and father
Luke and Nora Higgins
and my brothers
Joseph and John

With love

Acknowledgments

And so the good ship *Queen Charlotte* is ready to set sail. I hope all my readers will enjoy the voyage.

It is time once again to say a profound thank-you to Michael Korda, my editor of over forty years. He is, as always, indispensable. It was his suggestion that I set this story on a cruise liner, and he guided me through the process of completing it.

Marysue Rucci, editor-in-chief of Simon & Schuster, for her sage advice and creative suggestions.

My gratitude to my spouse extraordinaire, John Conheeney, who listens sympathetically when I am deep in the writing process. Hats off to my children and grandchildren, who are always encouraging and supportive.

A special note of appreciation to my son Dave for his research and editorial help.

Thank you to a gem of a jeweler, Arthur Groom, for spending time to walk me through the wonderful world of precious stones.

Many thanks to admiralty lawyer Jim Walker, who provided ideas about how ship management might respond to onboard emergencies.

Thank you to former FBI Special Agent Wes Rigler for his helpful advice.

I cannot fail to honor the memory of social arbiter Emily Post, who gave us a delightful glance at the customs and manners of one hundred years ago.

And last but surely not least, thank you, my dear readers. I so appreciate your continuing support.

Cheers and blessings,
Mary

ALL BY MYSELF, ALONE

Day One

1

The magnificent cruise liner *Queen Charlotte* was about to leave on her maiden voyage from her berth on the Hudson River. Promised to be the epitome of luxury, she was compared to both the first *Queen Mary* and even the *Titanic*, which had been the height of luxury one hundred years earlier.

One by one the passengers filed aboard, checked in and were invited to the Grand Lounge, where they were met by white-gloved waiters offering champagne. When the last guest had come aboard, Captain Fairfax gave a speech of welcome.

"We promise you the most elegant voyage you have ever or *will* ever encounter," he said, his British accent adding even more luster to his words. "You will find your suites furnished in the grand tradition of those of the most magnificent ocean liners of yesteryear. *Queen Charlotte* was constructed to accommodate precisely one hundred guests. Our eighty-five crew members are committed to serving you in every possible way. The entertainment will be worthy of Broadway, Carnegie Hall and the Metropolitan Opera. There will be a wide range of lectures to choose from. Our presenters include celebrity authors, former diplomats, and experts on Shakespeare and gemology. The finest chefs from around the globe will conduct farm-to-table cooking presentations. And we know that cruising is thirsty business. To remedy this hardship, there will be a series of wine tastings hosted by renowned connoisseurs. In keeping with the spirit of this cruise, one day there will be a lecture from the book of Emily Post, the legendary social arbiter of a century ago, illuminating the delightful manners of the past. These are only a few of the many activities you may choose from.

"In closing, the menus have been chosen from the recipes of the finest chefs the world over. Now, once again, welcome to your new home for the next six days.

"And now I would like to introduce Gregory Morrison, the owner of the *Queen Charlotte*. It was his vision that this ship would be perfect in every detail, and that is why you will enjoy the most luxurious cruise you will ever experience."

Gregory Morrison, a stout, ruddy-faced, silver-haired man stepped forward.

"I want to welcome all of you aboard. Today is the realization of a young boy's wish that began over fifty years ago. I stood next to my father, a tugboat captain, as he guided the most magnificent cruise ships of his day in and out of New York harbor. Truth be told, while my father was looking forward, toward where we were heading, I was looking back, watching in awe as spectacular cruise liners sliced elegantly through the gray Hudson River water. Even then I knew I wanted someday to build a ship even more awe-inspiring than the vessels I admired all those years ago. *Queen Charlotte* in all her majesty is the realization of the dream I dared to dream. Whether you are with us for five days to Southampton or stay with us for ninety days around the world, I hope today marks the beginning of an experience you will never forget." Raising his glass, he said, "Anchors away."

There was a smattering of applause, then people turned to their nearest fellow passengers and began to chat. Alvirah and Willy Meehan, celebrating their forty-fifth wedding anniversary, were relishing their great fortune. Before they won the lottery, she had been cleaning houses and he had been repairing overflowing toilets and broken pipes.

Thirty-four-year-old Ted Cavanaugh accepted a glass of champagne and looked around. He recognized some of the people on board, the chairmen of General Electric and Goldman Sachs, several Hollywood A-list couples.

A voice next to him asked, "By any chance would you be related to the ambassador Mark Cavanaugh? You bear a striking resemblance to him."

"Yes, I am," Ted smiled. "I'm his son."

"I knew I couldn't be wrong. Let me introduce myself. I am Charles Chillingsworth."

Ted recognized the name of the retired ambassador to France.

"Your father and I were young attachés together," Chillingsworth said. "All the girls in the embassy were in love with your father. I told him no one deserved to be that good-looking. He served as ambassador to Egypt for two different presidents as I recall, then to the Court of St. James's."

"Yes, he did," Ted confirmed. "My father was fascinated by Egypt. And I share his passion. I spent many years growing up there. Then we moved to London when he became ambassador to Great Britain."

"Have you followed in his footsteps?"

"No, I am a lawyer, but a good part of my practice is devoted to recovering antiques and artifacts that have been stolen from their countries of origin." What he did not say was that his specific reason for being on this voyage was to meet Lady Emily Haywood and persuade her to return her famed Cleopatra emerald necklace to its rightful owners, the people of Egypt.

Professor Henry Longworth overheard the conversation and leaned in closer to hear the exchanges better, his eyes sparkling with interest. He had been invited aboard as a lecturer. A renowned expert on Shakespeare, his presentations, which always included renditions of passages, never failed to delight his audiences. A medium-sized man in his sixties, with thinning hair, he was a sought-after speaker on cruises and at colleges.

Devon Michaelson stood a short distance apart from the other guests. He had no need or desire for the banal small talk that was the inevitable result of strangers meeting for the first time. Like Professor Longworth, he was in his early sixties with no outstanding height or remarkable facial features.

Also standing by herself was twenty-eight-year-old Celia Kilbride. Tall, with black hair and sapphire-blue eyes, she did not notice, nor would she have cared about, the admiring glances that were cast at her by her fellow passengers.

The first stop on the round-the-world voyage would be Southampton, England. That was where she would disembark. Like Professor Longworth she was an invited lecturer on the ship. A gemologist, her subject would be the history of famous jewels through the ages.

The most excited passenger in the room was fifty-six-year-old divorcée Anna DeMille of Kansas, who had been the grand-prize winner of this trip in a church-sponsored raffle. Her dyed black hair and matching eyebrows were bold against her thin face and body. Her prayer was that this would be her opportunity to meet Mr. Right. Why not? she asked herself. I won the raffle. Maybe this is finally going to be my year.

Eighty-six-year-old Lady Emily Haywood, famed for her wealth and philanthropy, was attended by the guests she had invited: Brenda Martin, her assistant and companion over the last twenty years, Roger Pearson, who was both her investment manager and the executor of her estate, and Roger's wife Yvonne.

When interviewed about the cruise, Lady Emily had stated that she intended to bring her legendary Cleopatra emerald necklace and wear it in public for the first time.

As the passengers began to disperse, wishing each other "Bon voyage," they could not know that at least one of them would not reach Southampton alive.

2

Instead of going to her cabin, Celia Kilbride stood by the railing of the cruise ship and watched as she sailed past the Statue of Liberty. Her time on the ship would be less than a week, but it was long enough to get away from the glaring media coverage of Steven getting arrested on the night of their rehearsal dinner, twenty-four hours before their wedding. Was it really only four weeks ago?

They had been toasting each other when the FBI agents walked into the private dining room of 21 Club. The photographer who had been taking pictures had snapped one of them together, and another focusing on the five-carat engagement ring she was wearing.

Handsome, witty, charming, Steven Thorne had cheated her friends into investing in a hedge fund that was created only to benefit him and his lavish lifestyle. Thank God he was arrested before we were married, Celia thought, as the ship sailed into the Atlantic. At least I was spared that.

So much of life is chance, she thought. It was shortly after her father died two years ago that she had been in London for a gemology seminar. When Carruthers Jewelers provided a business-class airline ticket, it was the first time she had flown other than in coach.

She was in her seat for the flight back to New York, sipping a complimentary glass of wine, when an impeccably dressed man put his briefcase in the overhead compartment and slid into the seat next to her. "I'm Steven Thorne," he said with a warm smile as he extended his hand to her. He explained that he was returning from a financial conference. By the time they landed, she had agreed to meet him for dinner.

Celia shook her head. How could she, a gemologist who could find a flaw in any gemstone, so misjudge a human being? She inhaled deeply and the wonderful scent of the ocean seeped into her lungs. I'm going to stop thinking about Steven, she promised herself. But it was hard to forget how many of her friends had invested money they couldn't afford to lose because she had introduced them to Steven. She had been forced to sit for an interview with the FBI. She wondered if they believed that she was involved in the theft, despite the fact that she had invested her own money in the scheme.

She had hoped not to know any fellow passengers, but it had been widely publicized that Lady Emily Haywood would be on the ship. She regularly brought pieces from her vast collection of jewelry to Carruthers on Fifth Avenue to be cleaned or repaired, and insisted that Celia check each one for any chips or scratches. Her assistant, Brenda Martin, was always with her. And Willy Meehan, the man who had come in to buy a forty-fifth wedding anniversary gift for his wife, Alvirah, had told her all about the fact that they had won forty million dollars in the lottery. She'd liked him immediately.

But with so many people on the ship, it would be easy to have plenty of private time, aside from the two lectures and one Q&A session she would be giving. She had been a guest speaker several times on Castle Line ships. Each time the agent in charge of entertainment events told her that the passengers had voted her the most interesting lecturer. He had phoned her only last week to invite her to fill in for a lecturer who had become ill at the last minute.

It had been manna from Heaven to get away from the sympathy of some friends and the resentment of the others who had lost money. I'm so glad to be here, she thought, as she turned and went down to her cabin.

Like every square inch of *Queen Charlotte*, the exquisitely furnished suite had been designed with meticulous attention to detail. It was a sitting room, bedroom and bath. It had roomy closets, unlike the older ships she had traveled on where the concierge suites were half this size. The door opened onto a balcony where she could sit outside when she wanted to feel the ocean breezes without being in the company of others.

She was tempted to go out on the balcony now, but decided to unpack and get settled instead. Her first lecture would be tomorrow afternoon and she wanted to go over her notes. The subject matter was the history of rare gems, beginning with ancient civilizations.

Her phone rang. She picked it up and heard a familiar voice on the other end of the line. It was Steven. He was out on bail before his trial. "Celia, I can explain," he began. She pressed End and slammed down the phone. Just hearing his voice made a wave of shame wash over her. I can detect the smallest flaw in any gem, she thought again bitterly.

She swallowed against the lump in her throat and impatiently brushed tears from her eyes.

3

Lady Emily Haywood, known to one and all as "Lady Em," sat straight-backed on a handsome wing chair in the most expensive suite on the ship. She was birdlike thin, with a full head of pure white hair and a wrinkled face that still held signs of beauty. It was easy to visualize her as the dazzling American prima ballerina who at age twenty had captured the heart of Sir Richard Haywood, the forty-six-year-old famous and wealthy British explorer.

Lady Em sighed and looked around. This is actually *worth* the money, she thought. She was sitting in the great room of the suite. It had a king-sized television set over the fireplace, antique Persian rugs, couches upholstered in pale gold tapestry on either end of the room, contrasting chairs, antique side tables and a bar. The suite also had a very large bedroom and a bath that included a steam shower and a Jacuzzi. The bathroom floor was heated, and incredible marble mosaics adorned the walls. Doors from the bedroom and the great room opened onto a private balcony. The refrigerator was stocked with the snacks she had chosen.

Lady Em smiled. She had brought some of her best jewels to wear on the ship. There were going to be a lot of celebrities on board for this maiden voyage, and as usual she wanted to outshine them all. When she signed up for the cruise, she had announced that in the spirit of her luxurious surroundings, she was going to bring with her, and wear, the fabulous emerald necklace that was believed to have belonged to Cleopatra. After the cruise, she was planning to donate it to the Smithsonian Institution. It's beyond priceless, she thought, and with no relatives I bother with, who would I leave it to? Besides that, the Egyptian government was trying to get it back, claiming it came from a looted tomb and must be returned. Let them and the Smithsonian fight about it, Lady Em thought. This is my first, and last, hurrah with the necklace.

The door to the bedroom was slightly open, and she could hear her assistant, Brenda, moving around inside it as she unpacked the steamer trunk and suitcases with the clothing Lady Em had chosen to bring from her extensive wardrobe. Brenda alone was permitted to handle Lady Em's personal possessions. Butlers and valets were not.

What would I do without her? Lady Em asked herself. Before I even *know* there is something I want or need, she anticipates it! I hope that her twenty years of devotion to me has not cost her the opportunity to have her own life.

Her financial advisor and the executor of her will, Roger Pearson, was another matter entirely. She had invited Roger and his wife on the cruise and always looked forward to Roger's company. She had known him since he was a boy, and his grandfather and father had been her trusted financial advisors.

But a week ago she had met an old friend, Winthrop Hollows, whom she hadn't seen in years. Like her, he had been a client of the Pearson accounting firm. When he asked if she still employed Roger, her friend had said, "Be aware he is not the man either his grandfather or father was. I would suggest that you have an outside firm review your finances thoroughly." When she pressed Winthrop for an explanation, he refused to say more.

She heard footsteps, then the door from the bedroom swung open. Brenda Martin came into the great room. She was a big woman, not so much overweight as muscular. She looked older than her sixty years because she wore her graying hair unflatteringly short. Her round face bore no trace of much-needed makeup. That face now registered a look of concern.

"Lady Em," she began timidly, "you are frowning. Is anything wrong?"

Be careful, Lady Em warned herself. I don't want her to know that I'm upset about Roger.

"Am I frowning?" she asked. "I can't imagine why."

Brenda's face now registered a look of profound relief. "Oh, Lady Em," she said, "I'm so happy that there is nothing disturbing you. I want you to enjoy every moment of this wonderful trip. Shall I phone and order tea?"

"That would be very pleasant, Brenda," Lady Em agreed. "I will be most interested to attend Celia Kilbride's lecture tomorrow. It's amazing such a young woman is so knowledgeable about gems. And I think I will tell her about the curse associated with the Cleopatra necklace."

"I don't think you ever told me about that," Brenda said.

Lady Em chuckled. "Cleopatra was taken prisoner by Caesar's adopted son and heir, Octavian. She knew that he was planning to take her on his barge to Rome as his captive and had ordered that she wear the emerald necklace during the voyage. As she was about to commit suicide, Cleopatra sent for the necklace and put a curse on it. 'Whoever takes this necklace to sea, will never live to reach the shore.' "

"Oh, Lady Em," Brenda sighed. "What a terrible story. Maybe you'd better just leave the necklace in the safe!"

"Not a chance," Lady Em said crisply. "Now let's order the tea."

4

Roger Pearson and his wife, Yvonne, were having afternoon tea in their suite on the concierge floor of the *Queen Charlotte*. With a hefty frame, thinning light brown hair and eyes that crinkled when he smiled, Roger was outgoing and gregarious, the kind of person who made everyone feel comfortable in his presence. He was the only one who dared to joke with Lady Em about politics. She was an ardent Republican; he was an equally passionate Democrat.

Now he and Yvonne looked at the list of activities for the next day. When they saw that Celia Kilbride was slated to speak at two-thirty the next afternoon, Yvonne raised her eyebrows. "Isn't she the one who works at Carruthers Jewelers and is involved in that hedge fund fraud?" she asked.

"That Thorne crook is trying to drag her into it," Roger said indifferently.

Yvonne frowned in thought. "I've heard that. When Lady Em brings any of her jewelry in to reset or repair, Celia Kilbride is the one she sees. Brenda told me that."

Roger turned his head to glance at her. "Then Kilbride is a salesperson there?"

"She's much more than that. I've read about her. She's a top gemologist and goes around the world selecting precious stones for Carruthers. She lectures on ships like this one to interest people with big bucks to invest in pricey jewelry."

"She sounds pretty smart," Roger observed, then turned to the television.

Yvonne studied him. As usual when they were alone, Roger dropped his hail-fellow-well-met demeanor and virtually ignored her.

She went back to sipping her tea and reached for a dainty cucumber sandwich. Her thoughts switched to the outfit she would wear tonight, a new Escada cashmere jacket and slacks. The jacket was in a black-and-white pattern and the slacks were black. The leather patches on the elbows of the sleeves gave the outfit the sporty look which was the dress code this evening.

Yvonne knew she looked far younger than her age, which was forty-three. She wished she was taller, but her figure was trim and the hairdresser had achieved exactly the shade of blonde that she wanted. Last time it had too much of a gold tint.

Her appearance was very important to Yvonne, as was her social status, the Park Avenue apartment and the house in the Hamptons. She had long ago become intensely bored with Roger, but loved their lifestyle. They didn't have any children, and there was no reason why Roger should be expected to pay college expenses for his widowed sister's three boys. Yvonne had been on the outs with his sister for years, but she suspected that Roger was paying the college bills for all of them anyway.

As long as that doesn't interfere with anything I want, she thought, as she finished the cucumber sandwich and swallowed the last of her tea.

5

"This is much too expensive, Willy, even if it is our forty-fifth wedding anniversary," Alvirah sighed as she looked around the suite Willy had booked to celebrate the occasion.

Even as she was protesting, Willy could hear the excitement in his wife's voice. He was in the living room area opening the complimentary bottle of champagne that had been chilling in a silver ice bucket. As he worked the cork open, he gazed at the floor-to-ceiling mirrors, and out at the dark blue waters of the Atlantic.

"Willy, we didn't need a room with our own balcony. We could go out on deck when we wanted to look at the water and feel the breeze."

Willy smiled. "Honey, on this ship I'll bet every suite has its own balcony."

Alvirah was now in the bathroom off their bedroom. And she was almost shouting. "Willy, can you believe this? There is a TV built into the bathroom vanity mirror. All of this must cost a fortune."

Willy smiled indulgently. "Honey, we get two million a year before taxes. We've been getting it for five years now and you also make money writing for the *Globe*."

"I know," Alvirah sighed, "but I'd much rather be using the

money to give to good causes. You know, Willy, 'much is expected from those to whom much has been given.' "

Oh boy, Willy thought. What's she going to say when I give her the ring tonight? He decided to give her a hint. "Honey, would you think about this? Nothing makes me happier than celebrating our lifetime together. It really hurts me if you don't let me show you how happy I've been with you for forty-five years. And I have something else I'm going to give you tonight. If you don't accept it, well, it will hurt me very much." Spoken like a politician, he thought.

Alvirah looked stricken. "Oh, Willy, I'm so sorry. Of course I'm glad to be here. And you know when you think of it, you were the one to say we're going to buy the lottery ticket that day. I said that we might as well have saved the dollar. I'm thrilled to be here and I'm thrilled with anything you may have to give me."

They were standing at the balcony door admiring the view of the ocean. Willy put his arm around her. "That's more like it, honey. And just think, for the next week we're going to enjoy every minute of every day."

"Yes, we will," Alvirah agreed.

"And you look beautiful."

Another expense, Alvirah thought. Her usual hairdresser was on vacation so she had had her hair dyed at a super-expensive salon. The suggestion of going there had been made by her friend Baroness von Schreiber, owner of the Cypress Point Spa, where Alvirah had gone right after she and Willy won the lottery. I should have known Min would only suggest that place, she thought, but she did have to admit that her hair was the soft shade of red she always liked. And Monsieur Leopoldo had shaped it becomingly. *And* she had lost fifteen pounds since Christmas and was able to again wear the really nice clothes Min had picked out for her two years ago.

Willy gave her a hug. "Honey, it's nice to know that on a ship like this the only thing you'll have to write about in your next column will be carefree cruising."

But even as he said it, Willy had a sinking feeling that things wouldn't turn out that way. They never did.

6

Raymond Broad, the butler appointed to Lady Em's suite, came in with a tray to remove the remnants of the afternoon tea. He had seen her leave, with her assistant trailing behind her, probably heading to the Queen's cocktail lounge on the seventh floor.

Only those with the fattest wallets can afford to be up there, he thought. The kind of people I really like. Expertly he placed the tea service and the leftover sandwiches and assorted sweets on the tray.

Next he went into the bedroom and looked around. He opened the drawers of the night tables on either side of the bed. So often rich people just dropped jewelry there instead of going to the safe in the closet. He watched for that.

And people can be careless about money too. If at the end of the trip someone left a bulging wallet in one of their drawers, they'd never miss a couple of hundred dollars that they didn't bother to count.

Raymond was very careful about what he stole, which was why no one had ever suspected him in the ten years he had been working for the Castle Line. And where was the harm in his making a little extra money feeding juicy tidbits to the tabloids about the antics of celebrities on board? He knew he was considered an excellent butler.

He went back into the great room, picked up the tray and left the suite. The smile of satisfaction that was always on his face after he had cased an area disappeared when he opened the door. Solemn-faced, trim in his uniform, his thinning black hair neatly combed over his bald spot, his expression became subservient, in case he met a guest in the hallway.

7

Professor Henry Longworth checked his bow tie to make sure it was exactly in place. Although the dress code for tonight was casual, he had no interest in wearing an open-neck shirt. He simply didn't like them. They reminded him of the shabby clothes he had worn during his rough and tumble boyhood in the slums of Liverpool. Even at age eight he had been shrewd enough to know that the only hope for his future would be achieved through education. After school, when other boys were playing football, or as the Americans call it, "soccer," he was studying.

At age eighteen he was awarded a scholarship to Cambridge. When he arrived there, his Scouse accent had been the subject of amusement to his fellow students. It had taken unceasing effort to completely eradicate it by the time he graduated.

Along the way he had developed a passion for Shakespeare, and eventually became a professor at Oxford, teaching that subject until his retirement. He knew his colleagues at Oxford had joked that when he died he would be laid out in his casket wearing a white tie and tails. But he didn't care.

The tie was straight and in perfect position under his shirt collar.

He put on his jacket, a lightweight plaid perfectly suitable for mid-September weather, and glanced at his watch. It was ten minutes before seven. Punctuality is the politeness of kings, he thought to himself.

His suite was on the concierge floor, and he had been pleasantly surprised that on this new liner the amenities were substantially more luxurious than the ones on older ships. Of course it was a joke to use the word "suite" for a bed/sitting room, but so be it. He walked over to the long mirror on the bathroom door and took a full-length glimpse of himself to be sure there was nothing amiss in his appearance. His reflection showed a thin sixty-year-old man, of medium height, wearing rimless glasses over intense brown eyes, with a bald head and a fringe of gray hair around it. He nodded approvingly, then went to the dresser to look over the passenger list again. Not surprisingly, celebrities from different walks of life were aboard. I wonder how many of them are complimentary guests of Castle Line. Quite a few, he imagined.

Since his retirement he had become a frequent lecturer on the line and was very popular with the cruise director. Six months ago, after reading the advance publicity of the maiden voyage of the *Queen Charlotte*, he had contacted the booking office and indicated that he would be pleased to be a guest lecturer on that voyage.

And here he was. With a warm feeling of satisfaction, Professor Henry Longworth left his cabin to go to the Queen's cocktail lounge and mingle among the most important passengers on board.

8

Ted Cavanaugh took a fleeting glance around his suite and then dismissed it. As the son of an ambassador, he was accustomed to luxurious surroundings. And even though these accommodations struck him as remarkably expensive, he was not going to waste any time enjoying them. Thirty-four years old, Ted had lived abroad with his parents until his college years, attending the international school in whichever country his father was posted. He was fluent in French, Spanish, and Egyptian Arabic. A legacy graduate of Harvard University, then Stanford Law School, his passion for antiquities traced back to his youthful years in Egypt.

Eight months ago, he had read that Lady Emily Haywood had signed on to the maiden voyage of the *Queen Charlotte*. He recognized the opportunity he would have as a fellow guest to find an occasion to plead his case to Lady Haywood. Cavanaugh intended to make clear to her that even though her father-in-law, Richard Haywood, had *bought* the necklace one hundred years ago, the evidence was overwhelming that it was a stolen artifact. If she gave it to the Smithsonian Institution and his law firm sued to recover it, it would generate unpleasant publicity for Lady Haywood and both her late husband and his father. The men were famed explorers, but his research indicated that they were guilty on several occasions of raiding ancient tombs.

That would be his pitch. It was well known that Lady Haywood took passionate pride in her husband's legacy. She might possibly listen to reason rather than have his reputation and that of his father sullied by a nasty lawsuit.

With this thought in mind, Ted decided that until cocktail time he would give himself the brief luxury of settling down with a book he had been wanting to read for months.

9

Devon Michaelson had scant interest in his surroundings. His luggage contained only the necessary clothing for this kind of trip. Behind his bland expression, his hazel eyes were alert and penetrating. He heard everything and missed nothing.

He was disappointed when he learned that the ship's captain and the chief of security had to be made aware of his presence on the ship. The fewer people who knew, the better, he thought. But if he was going to accomplish his mission, he needed the cooperation of Castle Lines to be placed at a table near Lady Emily Haywood's, where he could observe her and those around her.

The "Man with One Thousand Faces" was well known to Interpol. His brazen thefts, which had occurred in seven countries, were an embarrassment. His most recent heist, the theft of two early Henri Matisse paintings from the Musée d'Art de la Ville de Paris, had been only ten months earlier.

The thief liked to taunt Interpol about his accomplishments, often posting details about the crime in the weeks afterward. This time the thief had apparently taken a different tack. From an untraceable email account, someone claiming to be the Man with One Thousand Faces had posted his desire to own the Cleopatra necklace. The post appeared shortly after Lady Emily Haywood had foolishly bragged to the press that she would display it on this voyage.

Castle Lines had been aware of the threat when Devon contacted them. They quickly agreed to cooperate.

A non-social man, Devon dreaded the fact that he would be assigned to a table and have to make conversation with strangers, all of whom he was sure he would find intensely boring. But since Lady Haywood was only traveling as far as Southampton, that would be his final destination as well.

I've heard so much about the Cleopatra necklace, how perfectly matched the dazzling emeralds are and how breathtaking they are to behold. It would be interesting to see them close up, he thought.

His pretext for the trip, to share with his fellow passengers, was to scatter at sea the ashes of his mythical wife. A good cover story, he thought, one that would account for his wanting to spend periods of time alone.

It was nearly seven o'clock, the time when cocktails would be served in the exclusive Queen's Lounge, reserved for only those passengers on the private deck.

10

Anna DeMille gasped as she opened the door of her suite. Her previous experience at sea had been a Disney cruise. The only celebrities on board had been Mickey, Minnie and Goofy. That trip had not been fun because it was filled with families with young children, and one time when she sat on a lounge chair on a deck she had come in contact with a piece of chewed bubble gum that stuck to her new slacks.

But this! This was heaven.

Her luggage had been unpacked. Her clothes were on hangers in the closet or stacked neatly in the drawers. Her toiletries were arranged in the bathroom. She was delighted that the shower was also a steam bath and resolved to try it first thing in the morning.

She went around the suite inspecting every single item. The headboard of the bed was tufted with a flowered print which picked up on the edgings of the white coverlet.

She sat and bounced on the bed. The semi-firm mattress was exactly what she liked, and she saw that it could be raised to a seated position if she wanted to watch TV in bed.

She opened the door, stepped out onto the balcony and was disappointed to see that it was entirely private from the ones on either side. She had hoped that talking back and forth to the neighboring balconies would be a way to make friends.

She shrugged off that thought. There would be plenty of time to mingle at dinner and at all the social events. And she had a hunch that she would have luck getting started with a new man.

Divorced for fifteen years, she still remembered the exchange in court when the decree was finalized. Her newly ex-husband had said to her, "Anna, you are the most annoying person I have ever had the bad luck to meet."

Since then Glenn had remarried and had two children. His second wife was constantly on Facebook, gushing about her adorable husband and her perfect children. Sickening, Anna thought, but she did sometimes wonder what might have been if she and Glenn had had children.

"After all, tomorrow is another day" was her favorite expression from Scarlett O'Hara, her ideal woman. Her mind quickly turned to something infinitely more important than having missed any hidden qualities in Glenn.

What shall I wear tonight? She knew it was not a formal evening, but checked to be absolutely sure. Her new blue glen-plaid suit would be perfect, she decided.

With growing anticipation, she began her preparation for her first night on the *Queen Charlotte*.

11

At seven o'clock Celia debated about going to the Queen's cocktail lounge, but then decided that she would. Even though she wanted a lot of time to herself, she also realized that the downside would be having too much time to think. Of course there would be some people from the New York area on board, but certainly the majority of passengers would neither know nor care about Steven's hedge fund fraud.

The restaurant Steven had chosen for their first date was lovely. The maître d' had greeted him by name. Steven had arranged for them to have a quiet table in an alcove near the back.

He had complimented the earrings I was wearing. When I told him they had been my mother's, before I even realized it, I was sharing with him the story of losing both my parents.

Steven was so sympathetic. He said he rarely spoke about the tragedy in his life. He was also an only child. After his parents were killed in an automobile accident when he was ten, his loving grandparents had raised him in a small town twenty miles outside of Dallas. With a tear in his eye, he told me how his grandmother had died a few years earlier. She had been caring for his grandfather, who at the time was in the early stages of Alzheimer's. His grandfather, who no longer remembered him, was in a nursing home.

Steven shared with me a quote he had never forgotten. "I'm

fiercely independent, but I'm afraid of being alone." I had found a kindred spirit. I felt myself falling in love with Steven, falling in love with a lie.

She did not change from the light blue jacket and slacks she had worn aboard. A narrow gold necklace and diamond stud earrings and the ring that had been her mother's were the only jewelry she was wearing. She remembered what her father had said when he gave the ring to her on her sixteenth birthday.

"I know you can't remember her, but this is the first birthday gift I ever gave your mother, the year we were married."

She took the elevator up to the Queen's Lounge, and as she had expected, it was almost full. But there was a table for two that the waiter was clearing and she walked over to it. By the time she got there, it was ready, and in a moment a waiter was waiting to take her order.

She decided on a glass of Chardonnay, then began looking around the room, recognizing some celebrity faces. A voice asked courteously, "Are you expecting someone? And if not, may I share your table? The salon is busy and this seems to be the only seat available."

Celia looked up. A thin, balding man of medium height was standing there. His polite request had been delivered in a well-modulated tone of voice, with an unmistakable British accent.

"Of course you may," she said, forcing a smile. As he pulled out the chair, he said, "I know you are Celia Kilbride and will be lecturing on famous gemstones. And I am your fellow lecturer Henry Longworth. My subject is the Bard, Shakespeare, and the psychology of the characters in his plays."

This time Celia's smile was genuine. "Oh, I'm so glad to meet you. I loved studying Shakespeare in school and even memorized some of his sonnets." As the waiter returned with her Chardonnay,

Longworth waited, ordered a Johnny Walker Blue scotch on the rocks, then turned his full attention to Celia.

"And which was your favorite sonnet?"

" 'Thou art thy mother's glass . . . , ' " she began.

" 'And she in thee recalls the lovely April of her prime,' " Longworth finished.

"Of course, you know it," Celia said.

"May I ask, why is it your favorite?"

"My mother died when I was two years old. When I was about sixteen, my father recited it to me. And looking at her picture and mine, they're almost interchangeable."

"Then your mother must have been a very beautiful woman," Longworth observed matter-of-factly. "Did your father remarry?"

Celia felt the glistening of tears begin to form in her eyes. How did I ever get into this conversation? she asked herself.

"No, he never did." To forestall any more personal questions, she said, "He died two years ago."

The words still sounded unreal to her.

Daddy was only fifty-six, she thought. He never was sick a day in his life, but then he had a massive heart attack and was gone.

And if he were alive, he'd have seen right through Steven, she thought.

"I'm very sorry," Longworth said. "I know how painful that loss must be for you. Let me say that I am so glad that we are not speaking at the same time. I am very much looking forward to hearing your lecture tomorrow. Since I am a student of the wonderful Elizabethan era, tell me, do you cover any jewelry from that period?"

"Yes, I do."

"At your young age, how did you become such an expert?"

They were now on safe ground.

"I learned about gems from my father," she said. "From the time

I was three, what I wanted most for Christmas and birthdays was necklaces and bracelets for my dolls and me. My father was at first amused, and then realized I was fascinated by jewelry and began teaching me how to evaluate gems. Then after taking some geology and mineralogy courses in college, I went for my diploma in gemology and became an FGA, Fellow of the Gemological Association of Great Britain."

As the waiter arrived with Longworth's drink, Lady Em stopped at the table. She was wearing a triple pearl necklace and pearl earrings. Celia knew how valuable they were. Lady Em had brought them to Carruthers last month to be cleaned and restrung.

She began to get up, but Lady Em put a hand on her shoulder. "Please don't, Celia. I just wanted to say that I have requested that both of you be placed at my table in the dining room."

She glanced at Longworth. "I know this lovely young lady," she told him, "and I know your reputation as a Shakespearean scholar. It will be good to share your company." Without waiting for an answer, she swept past them with a man and two women in tow behind her.

"And who is that?" Longworth asked.

"That's Lady Emily Haywood," Celia explained. "She is a bit imperious, but I can assure you she's delightful company." She watched as Lady Em was escorted to a vacant table by the window. "She must have reserved that one," she said.

"Who are the people with her?" Longworth asked.

"I don't know the other two, but the larger woman is Brenda Martin, Lady Em's personal assistant."

"Lady Em, as you call her, seems to be rather authoritative," Longworth observed dryly, "but I don't regret being at her table. It should be quite interesting."

"Oh, I'm sure it will be," Celia agreed.

"Miss Kilbride." A waiter came up behind her. He was holding a phone in his hand. "A call for you," he said as he handed it to her.

"A call for me," Celia said, surprised. Don't let it be Steven again, she prayed.

It was Randolph Knowles, the lawyer she had hired when she was contacted by the FBI to give a deposition. Why would he be calling? she asked herself.

"Hello, Randolph, is there a problem?"

"Celia, I have to give you a heads-up. Steven has given a long interview to *People* magazine. It will come out the day after tomorrow. He claims you knew he was defrauding your friends. They called me asking for a comment. I declined. The article states that you and Steven laughed together about it!"

Celia felt her body go cold. "Dear God, how could he?" she breathed.

"Try not to be too upset. Everyone knows he's a congenital liar. My source in the U.S. Attorney's Office told me you are not currently a person of interest, but it is possible they will ask the FBI to interview you again about some of the information in the article. No matter what happens I'm afraid there is going to be some nasty publicity. A strong argument in our favor is that you invested a quarter of a million dollars in his hedge fund."

A quarter of a million dollars, the money her father had left her in his will. Every nickel she had.

"I'll keep you posted." He sounds worried, she thought. He's only a few years out of law school. I wonder if it was a mistake to hire him. He may be in over his head.

"Thanks, Randolph." She handed the phone to the waiter.

"Celia, you look troubled," Longworth said. "Is there anything wrong?"

"Try everything," Celia told him as the chimes indicated that dinner was being served.

12

Devon Michaelson was pleased to see that there was no available table in the Queen's Lounge and went down to the Lido Bar for a gin martini. He saw two well-appointed couples at the bar who fortunately were deep in conversation. When the chimes sounded, he went down to the dining room.

As on the *Titanic*, the first-class passengers dined in ultimate style. It was a smaller version of the most exclusive dining room on the *Titanic*. Decorated in Jacobean style, painted in peanut-white, the furniture, chairs and tables were oak and designed to add luxury and comfort at all times. Specially mounted chandeliers gave a regal look to the room. Candle-style lamps adorned each table. Silk curtains framed the large bay windows. An orchestra was quietly playing from a raised platform. Fine linen tablecloths set the tone for Limoges china and sterling silver utensils.

Michaelson would soon be followed into the dining room by a couple he judged to be in their sixties. As the three of them sat down, he extended his hand and said, "Devon Michaelson."

"Willy and Alvirah Meehan." The name struck a chord in Devon's memory. Where had he seen or heard of them? he asked himself. As they spoke, a second man came to the table. Tall, with dark hair, warm brown eyes and an easy smile, he took his place and introduced himself, "Ted Cavanaugh." A moment later a fourth guest arrived. "Anna DeMille," she announced in a loud voice. Devon judged her to be about fifty. She was very thin, with jet-black hair tapered to her chin, and fiercely black eyebrows, her smile wide and toothy.

"This is such an adventure," she exclaimed. "I have never been on a fancy cruise like this before."

Wide-eyed, Alvirah was looking around the dining room. "This is so beautiful," she said. "We've been on cruises, but I've never seen anything this spectacular. To think that people traveled like this. It takes your breath away."

"Honey, on the *Titanic* their breath was taken away. Most of the passengers drowned," Willy commented.

"Well, that's not going to happen to us," Alvirah said firmly.

She turned to Ted Cavanaugh. "In the reception area I heard you say that your father is the retired ambassador to Egypt. I've always wanted to go there. Willy and I were at King Tut's exhibit when it was in New York."

"It is quite a remarkable sight, isn't it?" Ted observed.

"I have always thought it a shame that so many of the tombs were looted," Alvirah said.

"I absolutely could not agree more," Ted replied emphatically.

"Did you see all the celebrities who are right here in this very room?" Anna DeMille asked. "I mean it's like being on the red carpet ourselves. Isn't it?"

No one answered as the first course was placed on the table. A generous heaping of Beluga caviar with sour cream on small triangles of toasted bread was served accompanied by tiny glasses of super-cold vodka.

After she dove into it, Anna turned her attention to Devon. "And what do you do?" she asked.

Devon's cover identity was that he was a retired engineer living in Montreal. That was not enough for Anna.

"Are you traveling alone?" she asked inquisitively.

"Yes, I lost my wife to cancer."

"Oh, I'm sorry. When did it happen?"

"A year ago. We were planning to take this trip together. I have brought the urn with her ashes to scatter into the Atlantic. It was her final request."

That should block off any more cross-examination, he thought. But Anna was not yet satisfied.

"Oh, are you going to have a burial ceremony?" she asked. "I've read that people do that. If you want company, I'll be happy to attend."

"No, I want to do it myself," he said as he moved his index finger under his eye to wipe away the beginning of a tear.

Oh, my God, he thought. There may be no getting rid of this woman.

Alvirah seemed to sense that he didn't want any more personal questions.

"Oh, Anna, tell me all about winning the trip," she said. "We won the jackpot in a lottery. That's why we're able to be here."

With Alvirah diverting Anna's attention away from him, Devon gratefully focused on the table to his right. He closely studied Lady Emily Haywood's pearls. Magnificent, he thought. But tinsel compared with her emeralds. A worthy challenge for the international jewel thief known as the "Man with One Thousand Faces." No expense had been spared to ensure he could stay close to Lady Em and the precious Cleopatra necklace.

He suddenly remembered what he had heard about Alvirah Meehan. She had been instrumental in solving a number of crimes. But it would be better if she didn't get involved this time. Between Alvirah and Anna, they could make my job harder, he thought grimly.

After the caviar, a small bowl of soup, a salad and a serving of fish, the main course choices were served. A suitable wine was offered with each course. After dessert, a small bowl, half-filled with water, was placed in front of each diner.

Willy looked at Alvirah pleadingly. Alvirah looked at Ted Cavanaugh and watched as he dipped his fingers in the bowl and dried them with the napkin in his lap, then moved the bowl and saucer to the left of his plate. Alvirah followed his example, and Willy followed hers.

"Is this what they call a finger bowl?" Anna asked.

I wonder what else we're supposed to call it, Devon thought to himself dryly.

"More dinners like this and I'll be big as a house," Anna sighed.

"You've got a long way to go." Willy smiled.

Anna turned her attention to Devon. As dinner was ending, she said, "I know there's entertainment in the ballroom tonight. Would you like to accompany me?"

"Thank you. But I don't think so."

"Well then, would you consider a nightcap?"

Devon stood up. "No," he said firmly.

He had intended to follow Lady Haywood's group if they went to watch the entertainment or into one of the ship's bars for a cocktail. He wanted to try to insinuate himself into her company. But that wouldn't happen with a type like Anna DeMille hanging on him.

"I'm afraid I have some phone calls to return. Good night, everyone."

13

At dinner Lady Em had introduced her guests to Professor Henry Longworth, then turned to Celia. "My dear, I know that you have met Brenda, but I don't believe you have met Roger Pearson and his wife Yvonne. Roger is my financial advisor and also the executor of my will, and of course, I hope I will not require his services in that area for many years to come."

Lady Em laughed. "I heard someone refer to me as a 'tough old bird,' and while not flattering, I believe it's true." If only it were true, she thought wistfully. They all laughed and lifted their wineglasses as Roger said, "A toast to Lady Emily. I know we are all honored to be with her."

Celia noticed that Henry Longworth raised his glass, but was somewhat taken aback by the all-inclusive toast. He hardly knows her, she thought. He was literally forced to join her and now he's supposed to be honored by her presence. Then when he looked in her direction and raised his eyebrows, she knew that was exactly what he was thinking.

When the caviar arrived, Lady Em looked at it with satisfaction. "Now this is the way caviar was served in the old days on a cruise."

"My guess is that in a restaurant you'd be paying two hundred dollars apiece for this much," Roger observed.

"For the price of this trip there should be a bowl of it," Brenda observed.

"Which doesn't mean we won't be enjoying it," Roger smiled.

"Brenda is so careful with my money," Lady Em said. "She wouldn't accept a suite next to mine. She insisted on going to the level below."

"And it's perfectly luxurious," Brenda said firmly.

Lady Em then turned to Celia. "Do you remember I once told you my favorite quote about jewelry?"

Celia smiled. "Yes, I do. 'People will stare. Make it worth their while.' "

Everyone at the table laughed.

"Very good, Celia. The famous Harry Winston told me that when I met him at a state dinner at the White House."

She explained to the others, "Celia is a gem expert. She's the one I consult when I buy jewelry or have any of my pieces checked for scratches or chips. Of course I enjoy wearing my best jewelry. What in heaven's name do you own jewelry for, except to wear it? Some of you may have read that on this trip I will be wearing the emerald necklace that was rumored to have been created for Cleopatra. My late husband's father bought it over one hundred years ago. I have never worn it in public. It is simply priceless. But it seemed fitting that with the majesty of this beautiful ship, I should wear it on the formal nights. On my return to New York I plan to donate it to the Smithsonian Institution. It is so exquisite that I want the world to see it."

"Is it true that there is a statue of Cleopatra wearing what is believed to be that necklace?" Professor Longworth asked.

"Yes, that is true. And, as I'm sure you know, Celia, emeralds in Cleopatra's time were not usually treated the way they are now to bring out every facet of their brilliance. The craftsman who treated these emeralds was far ahead of his time."

"Lady Em, are you sure you want to part with that necklace?" Brenda protested.

"I am. It's time to let the public appreciate it."

She turned to Henry Longworth. "When you lecture, do you recite any passages from Shakespeare?"

"Yes, I do. I select some and then ask the audience for particular ones they might like to hear."

"I'll be there in a front seat," Lady Em said emphatically.

They all murmured that they would be there as well, except for Roger's wife, Yvonne, who had no intention of listening to a lecture about Shakespeare.

A few minutes earlier she had spotted some people she knew from East Hampton; she excused herself and went to join them.

Captain Fairfax's table was in the center of the room. As dinner was ending, he stood up. "We do not usually serve a formal meal on the first night at sea," he said. "But we have made an exception. We wanted you to begin to experience the fascinating journey you will enjoy over the next five days. Our entertainment tonight is the opera singers Giovanni DiBiase and Meredith Carlino singing selections from *Carmen* and *Tosca*. I wish you a very pleasant evening."

"I would very much enjoy hearing them," Lady Em said as she stood up. "But I am a bit weary. I invite anyone who wishes to come join me for a nightcap in the Edwardian Bar."

Like Yvonne, Celia declined, explaining that she had to prepare for her lecture. Back in her suite she allowed herself to think about the possible consequences of Steven telling *People* magazine that she was involved in his theft.

He is such a liar, she thought. He was born lying. Everything he told me was a lie.

The press coverage immediately following Steven's arrest at their rehearsal dinner had left her shell-shocked. Then it got worse. His father, a wealthy oil and gas investor from Houston, called her and explained that Steven had been disowned by the family. He also said that Steven had a wife and child they were supporting in Texas.

Carruthers had spoken to her about taking a leave of absence when the scandal broke nearly a month ago. She had suggested, and they had agreed, that she would take several weeks of unused vacation time to allow matters "to sort themselves out."

Who knows what will happen after they see the article tomorrow? she wondered.

She did not sleep at all that night.

14

Yvonne and her friends enjoyed an after-dinner drink together in the Prince George Lounge. It was late when she returned to her suite, and Roger was not there. He probably couldn't wait to get to the casino, she thought. She was sure he had rushed down there as soon as Lady Em left for her room. He had always been a gambler, but now it was getting worrisome. She didn't care what he did with his time, just as long as he continued to support their lifestyle.

She was already in bed, but not yet asleep, when the door opened and he came in, smelling heavily of liquor.

"Yvonne," he said, his voice unsteady.

"Keep your voice down. You'll wake up the dead," she said sharply, then added, "Did you lose again tonight? I know you were dying to get down there."

"None of your business," he snapped.

On that cordial note, Roger and Yvonne Pearson finished their first evening aboard *Queen Charlotte*.

15

At Willy's suggestion he and Alvirah decided to skip the entertainment this evening. Instead he wanted to give Alvirah the ring he had bought her for their forty-fifth anniversary.

Back in their suite, he opened the bottle of champagne that had been their "Welcome Aboard" gift. He poured two glasses and handed one to Alvirah. "To the happiest forty-five years of my life," he toasted. "I could never live a day without you, honey."

Alvirah's eyes misted. "No more than I could live a day without you, Willy," she said fervently, then watched as he reached in his pocket for a small wrapped box. Now, don't tell him that he shouldn't have done it, and it was too much money, she warned herself.

When he handed the box to her, she unwrapped it slowly, then opened the lid to see an oval-shaped sapphire surrounded by small diamonds.

"Oh, Willy," she sighed.

"It's going to fit," Willy said proudly. "I brought along one of your other rings to be absolutely sure. You saw the gemologist who helped me select it at the next table tonight. She was that very pretty girl with the black hair. Her name is Celia Kilbride."

"Oh, I did notice her," Alvirah breathed. "How could you miss her? Wait a minute, isn't she the one whose boyfriend cheated everyone with his hedge fund?"

"Yes, she is."

"Oh, that poor girl," Alvirah exclaimed as she took a sip of champagne. "I've got to get to know her."

She slipped on the ring. "Oh, Willy, it's perfect, and I love it."

Willy let out a sigh of relief. She didn't ask me how much it cost, he thought. But it wasn't that bad at all. Ten thousand dollars. Celia told me it was one that a woman sold after her mother died. It would be worth much more, except that it has a scratch you can only see under a microscope.

Alvirah had a new thought. "Willy, that poor Devon Michaelson. I predict that Anna DeMille is going to try his soul. She heard that he has his wife's ashes to scatter into the ocean. My guess is that she'd love to toss them over for him. She's going to haunt him every day," Alvirah continued. "Of course, I can understand why she might want to get married again, and he's an attractive man. But she's going about it the wrong way."

"Honey, I beg you, don't start giving her advice. Stay out of it."

"I'd like to help, but you're right. However, I *do* intend to get friendly with Lady Emily. I've read so much about her."

Willy did not try to dissuade Alvirah this time. He knew perfectly well that by the end of the trip, Alvirah would be Lady Emily's new best friend.

Day Two

16

The 7 A.M. activity the next morning was a yoga class. Celia had
barely begun to doze but had forced herself to get up and attend.
About twenty people had shown up.

She was not surprised to see that the teacher was Betty Madison,
a famous yoga instructor who had written a bestselling book on the
topic. No amateurs on this ship, she thought, as she unrolled her
mat and settled in place. Nor on any of the other cruise ships on
which she had lectured. On those trips she had invited her close
friend Joan LaMotte to accompany her. This time she had not dared
to ask her. Joan and her husband had lost two hundred fifty thousand dollars in Steven's fund.

Same amount I lost, Celia thought, but I was the Judas goat who
led the lambs to slaughter.

There were so many signs, she thought. Why didn't I see them?
Why did I always give him the benefit of the doubt? Steven and I
enjoyed doing things together: museums, movies, theater, and jog-
ging in Central Park. When we did things with other couples, they
were always with *my* friends. His friends from his early years, he

explained, had stayed in Texas. And Steven believed it was good practice to not socialize with his work colleagues outside the office. "More professional" was how he described it.

With the benefit of hindsight it was abundantly clear why they hadn't socialized with Steven's friends. He didn't have any. The small number of his "friends" who came to the rehearsal dinner knew him from an evening basketball league he played in one night each week and from his workout class at the gym.

When the yoga session was over, Celia went back to her cabin and ordered breakfast. The ship's daily four-page news digest had been slipped under her door during the night. She feared that in the Wall Street section there might be an item about the interview Steven gave *People*. It would surely be a sensational piece of gossip. She opened it and was relieved to see that there was no mention of Steven.

But wait until tomorrow when *People* hits the stands. It was a recurrent thought, like a drumbeat in her head.

17

Captain Ronald Fairfax had sailed with the Castle Lines for twenty years. Every one of his ships had been top-of-the-line, but *Queen Charlotte* surpassed them all. Instead of following the lead of other cruise lines, like Carnival, building many supersized vessels that held more than three thousand passengers, on *Charlotte* the number had been limited to one hundred, far smaller than the old first-class ships had been.

That, of course, was why so many celebrities were on board, anxious to be counted as exclusive guests on the maiden voyage.

Captain Fairfax had gone to sea the day after he finished college in London. Tall, broad-shouldered, with a full head of pure white hair and a somewhat weather-beaten face, he was an impressive man. He was widely regarded as a superb captain and a marvelous host who walked easily among the most exalted guests.

Anyone in the know eagerly awaited an invitation to be a guest at his dinner table, or to be at one of his private cocktail parties in his beautiful and roomy suite. The invitations were kept for the crème-de-la-crème guests. Handwritten by the purser, they were slipped under the door of the recipients fortunate enough to make the cut.

None of this was on Captain Fairfax's mind as he stood on the bridge.

It was no secret that the expense of building and outfitting this extraordinary ship had ended up being nearly double the original projection. For that reason, it had been made clear to him by Gregory Morrison, the owner of Castle Lines, that absolutely no hitch was permissible. The tabloids and social media sites would be hungry for stories about anything that might go wrong on this all-important maiden voyage. They had already seized on the reference to the amenities of the *Titanic*. In retrospect, it had not been advisable to publicize the ship that way.

He frowned. There was already one indication that they might be sailing into a storm a day and a half out of Southampton.

He looked at his watch. He had an extremely confidential appointment in his quarters. The Interpol agent known to the other passengers as Devon Michaelson had requested a secret meeting.

What could Michaelson possibly want to speak to him about? He had already been told that the so-called "Man with One Thousand Faces" might well be on board.

He turned from the bridge and made his way to his suite. A few moments later there was a tap on the door. He opened it. He had identified Devon Michaelson by knowing he was at the same table as the ambassador's son, Ted Cavanaugh.

Fairfax extended his hand. "Mr. Michaelson, I cannot tell you how pleased I am that you are with us on this ship."

"I'm glad I am here as well," Michaelson said courteously. "As I'm sure you know, over the past several weeks the so-called 'Man with One Thousand Faces' has been dropping hints on various social media sites suggesting that he would be on this voyage. An hour ago he sent a message that he is on board, enjoying the luxurious surroundings, and stating that he was looking forward to adding to his jewelry collection."

Fairfax felt his body go rigid. "Is there any chance that someone may be putting out these messages as a joke?" he asked.

"I'm afraid not, sir. They have the ring of truth to them. And it is consistent with his track record. For him it is not enough to just steal what he wants. He derives extra pleasure from dropping hints about what he plans to do, and then poking his finger in the eye of law enforcement as he carries out his plan."

Fairfax said, "It is worse than I imagined. Mr. Michaelson, I think you can understand how important it is that this voyage must have no hint of scandal. Is there anything that I or my staff can do to help prevent a calamity?"

"I would say only be alert, as I shall be alert," Michaelson answered.

"Very good advice. Thank you, Mr. Michaelson," the Captain said as he walked him to the door.

Alone with his thoughts, Fairfax took comfort knowing that an agent was on board. Security Chief John Saunders and his team were very good at their jobs. Saunders had a fine reputation in the business and had served with him on previous Castle Line voyages. The security chief could deal discreetly with unruly passengers. Fairfax was confident that the ship's employees, from over fifteen countries, had been thoroughly vetted before they were hired. But the challenge posed by an international jewel thief was different.

The realization of what could go wrong weighed heavily on him as he made his way back to the bridge.

18

Like Celia, Yvonne went to the early yoga class. Nothing was more important than maintaining her trim figure and youthful appearance.

Roger had been asleep when she left but was gone when she returned to the suite. Probably chasing after Lady Em and hanging on her every word, Yvonne thought disdainfully.

She showered, ordered a light breakfast, slipped on a sweater and slacks and went to the spa. In advance, she had made appointments for several different types of massages and customized facials. These would be followed by late afternoon makeup sessions.

She was already becoming accustomed to the amenities on the ship. But even so, she was happily surprised by the beautiful appointment rooms and the treatment at the hands of the highly skilled estheticians. It was approaching lunchtime when she settled in a deck chair and was immediately tapped on the shoulder.

"I'm Anna DeMille," the woman to her left said to introduce herself. "But unfortunately no relation to Cecil B. DeMille. You remember him, of course, and the great story about him? He was directing a battle scene with hundreds of actors and was delighted with the way the scene went. Then he asked the cameraman, 'Did you get all that?' And the cameraman answered, 'Ready when you are, CB.' " Anna laughed heartily. "Isn't that a great story about my non-relative?"

Dear God, Yvonne thought, how did I get stuck with this one?

She forced herself to engage in a brief conversation, then stood up. "Nice chatting with you," she lied.

Seeing her leave, Anna turned to the woman to her right, who looked to be in her early sixties and had just closed her book.

"I'm Anna DeMille," she said. "This trip is so exciting. I would never be here except that I won the grand prize at my church's annual raffle. Imagine, an all-expenses-paid trip on the maiden voyage of the *Queen Charlotte*! I still can't believe it!"

"Very understandable."

Anna ignored the chilly tone in the woman's voice.

"What is your name?" she asked.

"Robyn Reeves," was the crisp reply, as the woman opened the book she had just closed.

Nobody is very talkative this morning, Anna thought. I'll take a walk and see if Devon is anywhere around. Poor man.

He must feel so alone being here by himself with his wife's ashes.

19

Yvonne had lunch with her friends Dana Terrace and Valerie Conrad in the small restaurant that was decorated as an English tea-room. They had mutually agreed that their husbands were welcome to make their own plans. The reason was that they wanted to gossip, and what they had to say would be boring to men.

"Hal is on the squash court," Dana announced.

"So is Clyde," Valerie said indifferently.

Yvonne did not say anything. There was no doubt Roger was in the casino. She was in secret awe of both Dana and Valerie. They both had the backgrounds that she longed for. Dana was a direct *Mayflower* descendant. And Valerie's father was not only well bred, but a successful investor.

Since childhood, she had had one goal in mind: marry well, not just for money, but also for social standing.

Yvonne's father and mother, both high school teachers, had thankfully retired to Florida after she graduated from her local state college. When she spoke of them, she promoted them to having been full-time college professors. Using her excellent command of French, she had taken one semester her junior year at the Sorbonne, and now referred to that as where she went to college.

Dana and Valerie had gone to the exclusive Deerfield Academy prep school and had been classmates at Vassar. Like Yvonne, they were in their early forties and very attractive. The difference was that they had always had a secure background, while she had to plan her way to the top.

Yvonne had met Roger Pearson when she was twenty-six and he was thirty-two. And he had fit the bill. Good-looking enough, at least when she had met him. Like his father and grandfather, a graduate of Harvard, and he also had been a member of the university's most exclusive clubs. Like them, he was a CPA. Unlike them it had turned out that he was not particularly ambitious. He liked to drink and was a gambler. Both of these traits he had kept carefully hidden. What he could not hide was the considerable paunch that he had developed over the almost twenty years they had been married.

It did not take long for Yvonne to see the real Roger, and that he was lazy. Five years ago, after his father's death, he had become president of the family's wealth management firm and had persuaded many of its clients, most importantly Lady Emily, to stay with him. She named him the new executor of her estate.

In Lady Em's presence Roger was a different person, speaking with authority about global finances, politics and the arts.

Together he and Yvonne kept up the appearance of a happily married couple and attended the social affairs and charity galas that they both loved. Meanwhile Yvonne had been on the lookout for a newly divorced successful man or—even better—a widower, but neither had appeared on her horizon. Her two best friends, Valerie and Dana, had both successfully remarried divorcés. She longed to join them.

Now over Prosecco and salads, they discussed the amenities of the ship and the people on it. Valerie and Dana knew Lady Haywood and, like everyone else, were in awe of her. The fact that Yvonne found her boring was fascinating to both of them.

"I've heard her twice-told tales, make that twenty-times-told tales, about her late great Sir Richard, more than I can possibly tell you,"

Yvonne confided, as she daintily removed a tomato from her salad. Why can't I remember to tell the waiter that I don't like tomatoes? she asked herself.

Valerie had a copy of the daily activities. "We can listen to a former diplomat who will dissect the history of troubled relations between the West and the Middle East."

"I could not think of anything *more* boring," Dana said as she took a large sip of her wine.

"Okay, we'll skip that one," Valerie agreed. "How about this? A master chef will demonstrate his quick and easy technique to add a gourmet touch to even the simplest meal."

"That might be interesting," Yvonne suggested.

"Valerie and I have live-in chefs," Dana explained. "We leave the cooking to them."

Yvonne tried again. "Here's one that might be fun: 'Emily Post's Classic Book About Etiquette: The manners of the nineteenth and early twentieth century.' Why don't we go? I'd love to hear about the way they did things in those days."

Valerie smiled. "My grandmother told me that my great-grandmother lived by the society rules of that time. Her first home after she was married was a brownstone on Fifth Avenue. At that time, people left calling cards with the butler. I understand that when my great-grandfather died, they draped the home with mourning cloth. The butler in his day clothes would answer the bell with the parlor maid standing close behind him until a footman secured black livery for the staff."

"My grandfather was one of the first to collect modern art," Dana said. "Emily Post referred to it as 'frightful things in vogue today with flamboyant colors, grotesque triangular figures and designs, that aside from novelty, are in bad taste.' My grandmother tried to make him throw them out. Thank God he didn't. They're worth millions today."

Yvonne added, "Well, if we're going to spruce up on our manners, let's start with that lecture. Maybe there'll be a section on the proper way to exit one marriage and enter another."

They all laughed. Valerie signaled the waiter and pointed to their almost empty glasses. They were quickly refilled.

"Okay," Dana said. "What other ones are they doing today?"

"There's the Shakespeare lecture," Yvonne volunteered.

"I saw that Professor Longworth was at dinner with you," Valerie said. "What is he like?"

"No barrel of laughs," Yvonne told her. "He has a habit of raising his eyebrows. I guess that's why his forehead is so wrinkled."

"How about Celia Kilbride?" Dana asked. "She's the one who is accused of being part of that hedge fund swindle. I'm surprised they invited her on this ship. I mean the way the Captain went on about everything being the best of the best. Why would they invite a crook to be here?"

"I read she claimed she was a victim too," Yvonne said. "And I know she's considered to be a very knowledgeable gemologist. "

"I should have had her look at my engagement ring from Herb," Valerie laughed. "It had been his grandmother's. If you squinted, you might get a glimpse of the diamond. When I got the divorce, I gave it back to him. I said, 'I wouldn't want to deprive some lucky woman of the chance to be adorned with this.' "

As they laughed, Yvonne thought both of them had married classy guys the first time, and they married big money the second time. I've got to keep my eyes open. Or better than that . . .

After they each took long sips from their glasses, Yvonne said, "I've got a mission for you two."

They looked at her expectantly. "Both of you dropped the guys you started with," she said. "Did you have another lined up?"

"I did," Valerie confirmed.

"So did I," Dana agreed.

"Well frankly, whatever existed between Roger and me is long since over. So keep your eyes open."

"Now, back to the lectures. So what's our schedule?" Valerie asked.

Dana answered. "I'm in the mood to be entertained. Let's go to all three: Emily Post, Shakespeare, and Celia Kilbride."

"To entertainment," Valerie said, as they clinked their glasses together.

20

Anna DeMille did not like to remember that she had started to drink the water in her finger bowl before she saw Ted Cavanaugh dip his fingers into his. She was pretty sure that no one had noticed, but the fact that someone might have continued to annoy her. That was why she opted to go to the lecture on etiquette. Maybe I can pick up some tips, she thought, no harm in that. And I can see that a lot of the people on this ship are pretty ritzy.

There was also the hope that Devon Michaelson might just happen to be there.

She waited to take a seat until the last moment before the lecture began, just in case he walked in and they could sit together.

That didn't happen. She did notice that Ted Cavanaugh, Professor Longworth and the Meehans were seated near the front.

I can understand why the Meehans might be here, she thought. But why would Cavanaugh and Longworth show up? she wondered.

Anna settled in next to an elderly gentleman who seemed to be alone. She was about to introduce herself and tell him her Cecil B. DeMille story, when the lecturer walked to the podium.

Julia Witherspoon was a severe-looking woman of about seventy. After introducing herself, she explained that she usually only spoke about dining etiquette. But on this voyage, it seemed appropriate to review the quintessential good taste of a century ago.

As Witherspoon began to speak, she had no way of knowing that Ted Cavanaugh was one of her most interested listeners. From the time he was a boy and had developed his love for Egyptian antiquities, he had also been interested in what constituted good manners in ancient times. He knew it would be a distraction to hear about the mores of society one hundred years ago, and he needed that distraction.

"Since what was known as etiquette a century ago is so disgracefully lacking today, you may be interested to hear about the beautiful customs that prevailed in the late nineteenth and early twentieth century.

"Let's start with wedding etiquette. When a young man gives his intended an engagement ring, he follows a tradition that began more than eighty years ago. The proper engagement ring is a solitaire diamond because it is the conventional example of, and I quote, 'the singleness and endurity of the one love in the groom-to-be's life.'

"At the first family dinner after an engagement, the girl's father would raise his glass and address the assembly by saying, 'I propose that we drink a toast to the health of my daughter Mary and the young man she has decided to add permanently to our family, James Manlington.'

"The young man should respond by saying, 'I, er . . . , we thank you all indeed for your good wishes. I don't think I have to tell you, the thing for me is to prove, if I can, that Mary has not made the mistake of her life by choosing me, and I hope that it won't be very long before we see all of you again at our own table with Mary at the head of it and I, where I belong, at the foot.' "

Witherspoon sighed. "What a shame that life is so rude today."

She cleared her throat. "And now to the wedding. The bride's gown should be white. Satin and/or lace are most appropriate.

"As for the bridal party, Emily Post put it this way: 'A distinguished uncle was asked, "Don't you think the wedding was too lovely? Weren't the bridesmaids beautiful?" '

" 'His answer was, "I did not think it was beautiful at all. Every one of the bridesmaids was so powdered and painted there was not a sweet face among them. I can see a procession just like them any evening on the musical comedy stage." ' "

Witherspoon went on to talk about the proper furnishings of a bride's home, including the necessary number of servants, the butler, two footmen, a cook with two kitchen helpers, a housekeeper and two maids.

She then proceeded to tell about how to garb a house for mourning.

By the time her lecture was over, there was no one in the audience who did not feel guilty of somehow making many a faux pas along the way.

As Witherspoon spoke, Ted Cavanaugh found himself only half-listening as his mind immediately returned to the challenge in front of him. Lady Haywood had finally told the truth, that she had the Cleopatra necklace that her husband had given to her. Whether she likes it or not, besides being famous explorers, Sir Richard and his father were tomb raiders, Ted thought. That necklace should have been on display all these years at the Museum of Cairo. She has no right to give it to the Smithsonian. If she does so, that will probably mean a protracted lawsuit to get it back. I could make a lot of money suing the Smithsonian, but I don't want that to happen.

I'm going to point out to her that if she doesn't want her husband and his father to be known as grave robbers, she should agree to turn the necklace over to the Cairo museum. Maybe I can convince her, he hoped. I'll certainly give it my best effort.

Ted Cavanaugh was not the only member of the audience who was not giving Witherspoon his full attention. Professor Henry Longworth made it a habit to attend the presentation that preceded his. It gave him a chance to size up the audience reaction, to see the type of material they responded to.

Longworth did not want to admit how eager he was to attend Witherspoon's lecture. He had never been able to lose the bitter memories of those poverty-stricken years in Liverpool, but even more so, of the ridicule he encountered when he first arrived in Cambridge. He had poured tea into his saucer at the first university dinner, raised it to his lips and slurped. Then he had caught the snickers and glances from the other students at the long table. The snickers broke into laughter when the student next to him poured his tea into his saucer and began slurping it too. Then the other students at the long table followed his example.

Henry could still hear their laughter pound in his ears. That was why he had studied etiquette as an avocation. And it had served him well. He knew his slightly aloof manner, as well as his compelling lectures, added to the air of mystery he had created for himself.

What others did not know was that he owned a home in Mayfair that he had bought long ago when prices were affordable. He had carefully studied magazines that showed society homes, and little by little, he had turned his home into a paragon of good taste. Year by year he had furnished it with beautiful objects collected while speaking on tours. Only his cleaning woman knew it existed. Even his mail was sent to a post office box. The house and the furnishings were his. In his smoking jacket he would sit in the library, and as his eyes moved about the room, one by one he would enjoy and relish a beautiful painting or a fine piece of sculpture. In that room he truly became himself, "Lord" Henry Longworth. It was the fantasy world that had become his reality. And after a trip he was always happy to return there.

He listened as Anthony Breidenbach, the entertainment director, announced that his Shakespeare lecture would begin after a fifteen-minute recess. At three-thirty, gemologist Celia Kilbride would present.

21

Celia was gratified to see that Lady Emily, Roger Pearson and Professor Henry Longworth were in the first row of the auditorium. Not only that, but the occupants of the table next to hers at dinner last night were there as well.

She had about the same number of people in the audience as Longworth had had. The moment before she began to speak, she felt a wave of nervousness paralyze her, as usual. And then it was gone.

"A lecture about the history of jewelry should begin by defining the word itself. Jewel is derived from the French word 'j-o-u-e-l,' which roughly translates to 'plaything.'

"Although early man created jewelry out of shells and other objects, the first use of jewelry from a precious metal almost certainly involved gold. It's easy to see why gold was such a natural choice. It is widely dispersed throughout the world, and early societies had an easy time collecting the shiny metal from streambeds.

"Gold had the advantage of being very easy to work with. Early societies noticed that it neither tarnished nor corroded. This sense of permanence quickly led to it being associated with the gods and immortality in many cultures and in ancient texts. The Old Testament made reference to the Golden Calf, and Jason and the Argonauts searched for the Golden Fleece around 1200 B.C.

"The constant theme of Middle Eastern kingdoms was the desire for gold. The king of Babylon wrote, 'As for gold, send me what you have to hand as quickly as possible.'

"The king of the Hittites wrote in a letter, 'Send me great quantities of gold, more gold than was sent to my father.'

"The most abiding image of ancient Egypt is reflected in gold because it is considered the material of the flesh of the gods and the color of divinity."

Over the next twenty minutes she spoke of the evolution of jewelry and when various precious gemstones came into use.

Celia had decided that since Lady Em had openly admitted that she was in possession of the Cleopatra necklace and would be wearing it on board, she would relate the story of the necklace as well as the other fantastic jewels that had adorned Cleopatra during her thirty-nine years of life. The audience's rapt attention confirmed that she had made the right choice.

She regaled them with stories about ancient Egyptian jewelry in general including the ornaments for the head and neck, the collars and girdles adorning the body, the bracelets, finger rings and anklets for the arms and the legs.

What she did not know was that her most attentive listener in the audience was a person who already knew the history of all the gems she had mentioned and was silently congratulating her for the accuracy of her presentation.

She told the audience that her second lecture would include a focus on the unique role of the emerald in the history of jewelry. Then she would speak about the history of legendary diamonds like the Koh-i-Noor diamond that was now in Queen Elizabeth's state crown and the Hope Diamond, which was donated to the Smithsonian.

Celia finished her lecture by saying, "Lady Emily Haywood, who is here today, is the current owner of the priceless Cleopatra necklace, and I understand that she is planning to wear it on this voyage before she donates it to the Smithsonian Institution upon her return to New York. Like the Hope Diamond, it will be seen by millions of viewers every year."

Lady Em stood up. "Celia, you must tell the story about the legend of the curse on the Cleopatra necklace."

"Are you sure you want me to, Lady Em?"

"Absolutely."

Hesitantly, Celia explained the curse. "After being ordered to wear the necklace at sea while being taken prisoner to Rome, Cleopatra put a curse on it: 'Whoever wears this necklace to sea will not live to reach the shore.' " She quickly added that legends by their very nature are not based on truths, and she was sure that this was the case with the Cleopatra necklace.

From the applause, Celia knew that her lecture had gone over very well. Quite a few people came up to her to say how much they had enjoyed it, and three women asked if antique jewels they inherited might have more value than they had realized.

She always had the same answer to that question. "When you return to New York, bring any jewelry you want appraised to me at Carruthers and I'll be happy to evaluate your pieces."

One woman who appeared to be in her late sixties would not take no for an answer. She was wearing a ring on the third finger of her left hand.

"Isn't this a glorious diamond?" she asked. "My new gentleman friend just gave it to me before we sailed. He told me it's four carats and was mined in South Africa only last year."

Celia dug into her pocketbook and took out the small eyepiece known as a loupe. She held the loupe to her eye as she examined the ring. At a glance Celia could see that the stone was zirconium. She said, "Let's go over to the window so I can see it in a better light." With a smile and a thank-you to the women around her, Celia walked to the window.

"Are you traveling with friends?" she asked casually.

"Oh yes, I am. Four of my friends and we call ourselves the 'Sail Away Widows.' We go all over the world together. Of course we all agree that it would be much nicer to be with our husbands, but it is what it is and we have to make the best of it."

"But you said you have a boyfriend," Celia said.

"Oh I do. He's ten years younger. I'm seventy, but he said he's always dated older women. He's divorced."

"I'm sorry. I don't think I asked your name," Celia said.

"Oh, I'm Alice Sommers."

"Where did you meet your gentleman friend?" Celia asked, trying to make it sound like a casual question.

A blush came over Alice Sommers's face. "I know you might think it's silly, but just for fun, I joined that online dating service You and I Together, and Dwight responded to my profile."

Another con artist, Celia thought, and judging by the way the four widows are able to readily travel, they are pretty well off.

"Alice," Celia said, "I'm going to be honest. This is not a real diamond. It's zirconium. Although it looks nice, it's worth nothing. This isn't easy to tell you and you'll probably feel hurt and embarrassed because that's the way I felt. My fiancé bought me a beautiful engagement ring, but then I learned that he was tricking people into investing in his hedge fund and had used that money to, among other things, buy that ring. My advice is to throw your ring in the ocean and enjoy the friends who travel with you."

Alice Sommers listened. For a moment she was silent, then she bit her lip. "I feel like a fool," she said. "And my friends were trying to warn me! Celia, would you go out on the deck and watch me throw this piece of garbage overboard?"

"I'll be happy to do that," Celia said with a smile. But even as she followed Alice outside, she realized that she had given her a good tidbit to gossip about. One of them would research her name online and get all the details of her involvement with Steven. And in the way of the world, that situation would go through the ship like wildfire.

No good deed goes unpunished, she thought, as a minute later, Alice Sommers, with a game smile, took the zirconium off her finger, tossed it high in the air and watched it disappear into the increasingly choppy waters.

22

Willy and Alvirah had attended the Shakespeare and etiquette lectures, and Celia's. Afterward, they went outside to take a walk on the deck.

Alvirah sighed, "Oh Willy, wasn't it interesting to hear about the social customs of one hundred years ago? Then Celia's stories about the jewelry were so fascinating. And when Professor Longworth recited those sonnets from Shakespeare, it made me wish I had learned them when I was young. I mean, I feel so uneducated."

"You're *not* uneducated," Willy said fervently. "You're the smartest woman I know. I bet a lot of people would love to have your common sense and your ability to judge people."

Alvirah's expression brightened. "Oh Willy, you always make me feel so good. But speaking of judging people, did you notice that Yvonne Pearson took off like a bird after dinner last night? She didn't wait for anyone else to even get up."

"No, I didn't pay any particular attention to her," Willy said.

"Well, I saw her go over to another table and start kissing the people at it. I thought that as Lady Haywood's guest, it was very rude to leave ahead of her."

"I suppose so," Willy agreed. "But it doesn't matter. Does it?"

"Something else, Willy. I like to consider myself a student of human nature. My guess is that there is no love lost between Roger and Yvonne Pearson. Even though we were at the next table, I could see that they were ignoring each other.

"But you know who I think is charming? That nice young man, Ted Cavanaugh. And I am so sorry for that beautiful girl Celia Kilbride. To think of what that snake of a fiancé did to her. By the way, Ted was not wearing a wedding ring. At the table I was glancing between him and Celia Kilbride. I was thinking what a good-looking couple they would make. And what gorgeous children they would have."

Willy smiled.

"I know what you're going to say, Willy. 'Matchmaker, matchmaker, make me a match.' And Willy, did you notice the other woman at Lady Em's table? I mean Brenda Martin, Lady Em's companion. She's kind of a big lady, with short, gray hair."

"Oh, sure, I noticed her," Willy agreed. "She's no beauty."

"You're right about that. Poor thing. But I fell in step with her when I was taking a walk this morning when you were doing the crossword puzzle. Anyway, we started chatting. At first she didn't say much, but then she began to open up. She told me that she's been working for Lady Em for twenty years and goes all over the world with her. I said, 'That must be fascinating.' Then she laughed and said, 'Fascination wears thin,' *and* she told me that they had just come back from spending the summer in East Hampton."

"Well, you sure got all of them down pat," Willy observed as he drew in a deep breath. "I love the smell of the ocean. Remember how we used to go down to Rockaway Beach on Sundays during the summer?"

"I do. And you can bet there isn't a finer beach, including the Hamptons. Anyway the traffic in the Hamptons is terrible, but I still like those bed-and-breakfasts we've stayed at out there. Brenda told me that Lady Em has a mansion in the Hamptons."

"Is there anything Brenda *didn't* tell you?" Willy asked.

"No, that was it. Oh, yes. When I said, 'Brenda, you must love staying at a mansion,' her answer was 'I'm bored stiff.' Isn't that a funny thing to say about your employer?" Alvirah shook her head. "Willy, reading between the lines, I get the feeling that Brenda is sick of being at Lady Em's beck and call. I mean she made remarks like 'Lady Em is reading a book and told me I could take a walk for an hour. *Precisely one hour.*' Doesn't that sound to you as if Brenda is on call 24/7 and doesn't like it a bit?"

"It sounds like it," Willy agreed. He added, "I wouldn't like it either. On the other hand, why would Brenda change jobs at this stage of the game? Lady Em is eighty-six years old, and not too many people live a heck of a lot longer than that."

"Oh, I agree," Alvirah said quickly. "But I do get the impression that Brenda Martin is really fed up with Lady Em. I mean in a really serious way."

23

Celia did not go down to dinner. She spent the rest of the afternoon reading in a lounge chair on her private balcony.

On the one hand it was a good way to unwind after her lecture; on the other it was hard to get into a book. Her concentration was constantly interrupted by the same thought. Suppose the U.S. Attorney's Office decides to indict me after all? I don't have any money to keep paying a lawyer.

The management at Carruthers had been sympathetic until now, but when the article in *People* comes out, it is likely that they will fire her, or at least ask her to take an unpaid leave of absence.

At six o'clock she ordered dinner, a salad and salmon. Simple as it was, she could not finish it. When she had come back to the suite, she had changed into slacks and a shirt, but now she decided to put on pajamas and go to bed. Suddenly very tired, she remembered that she had not slept at all the previous night.

Before the butler came in to turn down the bed, she put a QUIET PLEASE sign on the doorknob. I guess that sounds friendlier than DO NOT DISTURB, she thought wryly.

She fell asleep immediately.

24

The formal dress code for dinner was in effect, so the men were in black tie and the women in cocktail dresses or gowns. The talk at Alvirah and Willy's table was of the three lectures and how entertaining they had been.

A few feet away Lady Em waxed eloquent on Sir Richard's ancestral home. "It was quite splendid," she said. "Think of Downton Abbey. Of course, after World War I, things became simplified. But my husband told me that in his father's time, there was a full staff of twenty servants.

"Everyone dressed for dinner. And on weekends the house was always filled with guests. A number of times 'Prince Bertie,' as he was known, attended. As everyone knows, after King Edward VIII gave up the crown, Bertie became King George VI, Queen Elizabeth's father."

Of course he did, Yvonne thought, but managed to keep an attentive smile on her face.

After dinner Lady Em decided to go directly to her suite. But when Roger offered her his arm, she said, "Roger, I would like to have a quiet meeting with you tomorrow morning at eleven o'clock in my suite. Come alone."

"As you wish, Lady Em," Roger agreed. "Is there anything special we need to discuss?"

"Why don't we talk about it in the morning?" she suggested.

When he left her at the door, she did not realize how her casual request had so deeply troubled Roger.

25

At the end of dinner Devon Michaelson had decided that it would be a good idea to cement his identity in the eyes of his table-mates, Ted Cavanaugh, the Meehans, and Anna DeMille—namely that he was a widower traveling on the ship with the sole purpose of scattering his late wife's ashes into the ocean.

"I have decided to drop them from the uppermost deck at eight a.m. tomorrow morning," he announced. "In thinking about it, I decided I would like to share the ceremony with all of you. Alvirah and Willy, you are celebrating your forty-fifth wedding anniversary. Anna, you are celebrating winning the church raffle. Ted, I don't know if you are celebrating anything, but you are also welcome to come. In my own way I am celebrating thirty years of happiness with my beloved Monica."

"Oh, I'll be there," Anna DeMille said fervently.

"Of course we'll be there," Alvirah said gently.

Devon turned his head as though he were blinking moisture from his eyes. Instead he was taking in the ruby-and-diamond necklace and matching earrings Lady Em had chosen to wear that evening.

Very nice, he thought, very, very expensive, but nothing like the Cleopatra necklace.

He turned his attention back to his own table. In a husky voice, he said, "Thank you. You are all very kind."

26

Yvonne went straight to their suite as Roger escorted Lady Em to hers. When he entered, Yvonne was in a miserable mood. Dana and Valerie had left with other friends and had not invited her to join them.

She sailed into Roger. "I can't stand listening to that insufferable old witch for five more minutes. She doesn't own you. Tell her you work for her Monday through Friday. Period."

Roger let her finish her tirade and then began shouting back. "You think I like having to kiss that old bag's feet? I have to inflate every bill to keep you in the lifestyle you've managed to become accustomed to. You know that as well as I do."

Yvonne glared at him. "Will you please keep your voice down. They can hear you on the bridge."

"And you don't think they can hear *you*?" Roger shot back, but he did lower his voice.

"Roger, will you please tell me why you—" Then she noticed that he was sweating profusely and his complexion was a grayish pallor. "You look sick. What's wrong with you?"

"What's wrong is that Lady Em wants to see me tomorrow morning alone in her suite."

"So what?"

"I think she suspects something."

"Suspects what?"

"That I've been cooking her books for years."

"You what?"

"You heard me."

Yvonne stared at him. "You're serious?"

"Oh, I am, my dear, I am."

"And if she does suspect, what would she do about it?"

"Probably when she gets back to New York, hire another accounting firm to go over them."

"And what would that mean?"

"Try twenty years in federal prison."

"You're serious!"

"Dead serious."

"Then what are you going to do about it?"

"What are you suggesting, that I throw her overboard?"

"If you don't, I will."

They stared at each other, then Roger, his voice shaking, said, "It may come to that."

27

Alvirah and Willy were passing Roger and Yvonne's suite and could not help but hear that they were shouting at each other. Alvirah immediately stopped to catch every word. The last words she caught were "federal prison," before another couple came down the hallway and she was forced to keep moving.

The minute Willy closed the door of their suite she turned to him, "Willy, did you hear all that? They hate that poor old woman."

"I heard more than that. I think he's stealing from her. The last words I heard were 'twenty years in a federal prison.' "

"Willy, I'm telling you, I think that they're desperate. And I think that she's even more desperate than he is. Do you think it is possible that either of them would try to hurt Lady Em?"

28

Professor Henry Longworth felt the tension at Lady Em's dinner table and excused himself from having an after-dinner cocktail. Instead, he went straight to his suite and made some notes on his computer.

It did not take him long. He wrote about the hostility lurking beneath the surface at the table and the furtive glances at Lady Em's jewelry by someone at the next table. These facts would serve him well. Very interesting, he thought with a smile.

Then for an hour he watched the news. Finally, before he went to bed, he thought about Celia Kilbride. The telephone call she had received in the cocktail lounge yesterday intrigued him enough to now search the Internet for information about her. What he found was a revelation. The beautiful young gemologist may or may not have been involved in a fraud, he read, although she had not been indicted.

Who would have guessed? he asked himself, somewhat amused. On that thought, he decided to go to bed. For about half an hour he did not sleep. In his mind he was anticipating the Captain's cocktail party. Would this be the occasion where Lady Em would wear her Cleopatra necklace, *her priceless emerald necklace . . .*?

29

Captain Fairfax was in bed in his suite. A creature of habit, he knew that reading for twenty minutes before going to sleep relaxed him. He was moments away from turning off the reading lamp when his phone rang. It was the ship's chief engineer.

"Captain, we are experiencing some propulsion issues. They are minor and we are conducting tests on each of the engines. We expect to have the issue resolved over the next twenty-four hours."

"Was it necessary that the ship slow down?"

"Yes, sir. But we can maintain a speed of twenty-five knots."

Fairfax began doing a calculation in his head. "Very well. Keep me posted," he said as he hung up the phone.

The Captain thought of the beehive of activity that awaited them at Southampton. A small army of cleaners would be standing ready to thoroughly clean the ship and make ready for the new passengers who would board. New provisions would be brought on and trash would be removed. All this would happen in the brief window between passengers disembarking in the midmorning and new guests coming aboard in the midafternoon. The process functioned like clockwork. But the clock had to start on time, with *Queen Charlotte* arriving by 6 A.M. in Southampton.

We'll be okay, he tried to assure himself. We can make up the time we will lose over the next twenty-four hours by going faster after the engine problem is resolved. We'll be fine, as long as nothing else happens to delay our arrival.

Day Three

30

Celia was surprised when she woke at 7:30 A.M., so early. What did you expect? she asked herself. You were in bed at eight-thirty last night so you've had eleven hours' sleep. She still felt as if the weight of the world were on her shoulders. Oh, come on, she decided, get with it! Take a walk. Clear your brain.

Acting on her decision, she dressed quickly in Lululemon and sneakers and went up to the promenade deck. She was surprised to see Willy and Alvirah standing there.

She was about to pass them with a friendly wave, but Alvirah was having none of it. "Oh Celia," she said, "I want to get to know you. I know you helped Willy pick out that beautiful sapphire ring for me. I've never had anything nicer."

"I'm so glad you like it," Celia said sincerely. "Your husband was so hoping that you would."

"Oh, I know what you mean," Alvirah said. "He was probably sure I would say it was too expensive. Did you know that Devon Michaelson is going to throw his wife's ashes into the ocean? He asked the people at his table to join him for a little ceremony."

"Oh, then I'll get going," Celia said.

But she was too late. Before she could resume walking, Michaelson had come up to them.

"I told Celia why we're here," Alvirah said.

Michaelson was holding the silver urn in both hands. "I've been intending to tell you how much I enjoyed your lecture, Miss Kilbride."

"It's Celia. Thank you. This must be a difficult moment for you. When my father died two years ago, I took his ashes up to Cape Cod and gave them to the ocean as well."

"Were you alone?"

"No, some close friends were with me."

"Then perhaps you will join me, along with my friends from the table?"

Devon Michaelson's expression was that of a man devastated. Celia felt a wrench of pity. "Of course, if you would like me to stay."

It was only a minute later that Ted Cavanaugh and Anna De-Mille joined them.

"Oh, it's chilly," DeMille said. "I should have worn a warmer jacket. But it doesn't matter," she added quickly. "We all want to be here with you, Devon." She patted his shoulder with tears in her eyes.

She's trying to be the chief mourner, Alvirah thought. She glanced at Willy, who nodded to let her know that he was aware of what she was thinking.

"I thank all of you for being with me today," Devon began. "I want to spend a few moments telling you about Monica. We met in college in London thirty-five years ago. Some of you may understand what love at first sight is all about."

Alvirah glanced at Willy to signify, "We do."

Anna DeMille's expression was focused adoringly on Devon Michaelson. He was saying, "I'm not a singer, but if I were, the song I would select would be Monica's favorite, from the movie *Titanic*, 'Nearer My God to Thee.' "

"I couldn't help but overhear as I was passing." Chaplain Kenneth Baker had paused at the group. He looked at Devon. "May I bless the urn with your wife's ashes?"

Alvirah could see that Devon Michaelson's expression was startled, his face crimson-red and his voice hesitant before he said, "Of course, Father, thank you."

In a low voice, Father Baker said the words of the Christian burial, finishing with, "May the angels receive you. Amen."

Before Devon could turn and lift the urn high to scatter the ashes into the sea, Alvirah could see how his face had become. It's not that he's sad, she thought. He's embarrassed because Father Baker asked to bless the urn. The big question is, Why?

They watched as Devon opened the urn and turned it over. The ashes danced in the breeze before descending and disappearing into the swiftly moving wake.

31

Lady Em began choosing the jewelry she'd wear tonight to the Captain's cocktail party.

"I think I'm going to wear the Cleopatra necklace tonight," she told Brenda. "I was planning to wear it for the first time to dinner with the Captain tomorrow night, but why not tonight as well? I've had it for fifty years and have never worn it in public."

Her eyes became dreamy as she remembered intimate dinners with Richard as he recounted the story about his father's purchase of the necklace. She looked up at Brenda. "What do you think?"

"Why not?" Brenda asked indifferently, then caught herself. "Oh, Lady Em, what I mean is that you have so few opportunities to wear it, why not display your necklace on several occasions on the ship, especially since, thanks to Celia Kilbride's lecture, everyone will be fascinated to see it?"

"And perhaps to see if the Cleopatra curse will be fulfilled in the next few days," Lady Em observed dryly, then wondered why a chill went through her body.

"Absolutely not," Brenda said firmly. "I've been with you twenty years, Lady Em, and I never heard you say anything like that. And I have to tell you, I don't like hearing you talk like that. I've never seen the Cleopatra necklace, but already I don't like it."

"The only ones who have seen it in the last one hundred years are my husband, his father and I," Lady Em said.

Brenda had sounded so passionate and sincere in expressing her concern that Lady Em chided herself for her suspicion that there was something in her longtime assistant's attitude that was anything but loyal. I'm so upset about the situation with Roger that maybe I have been brusque with her the last few days, she thought, and that certainly isn't fair to her.

They had pouches of jewelry on the bed and she began opening them one by one. The first one contained the pearls, earrings and ring she had worn the first night on board. They're probably the next most valuable pieces, Lady Em observed. "Brenda, I know I may have told you how the twenty-one-year-old wife of the great opera singer Caruso wrote a memoir about her life with him. In it she wrote of going to Delmonico's after the opera and having everyone who mattered come up to their table to pay homage to him. In the memoir she wrote, 'And I was wrapped in sable, pearls and enchantment.' "

"I think you did tell me," Brenda replied to her employer gently.

"Oh, I'm sure I did," Lady Em agreed cheerfully. "I suppose it's that as you get older you talk about the past more and more." She held up a diamond bracelet. "I haven't worn this in years. The very expensive jewels I brought to wear on the cruise were the pearls I wore the night we sailed, the ruby-and-diamond necklace, and of course, the emerald necklace. That I'll wear tonight. But I love this bracelet. Richard picked it up for me one morning when we were walking past Harry Winston on Fifth Avenue. We stopped to look at the window display and I happened to admire it. Richard propelled me inside and a moment later it was on my wrist. He paid eighty thousand dollars for it. When I protested, he said, 'It isn't that expensive. Wear it to picnics.'

"Dear God, how he pampered me. But he also was the most generous man alive. He contributed to so many charities." Her expression changed as she examined the bracelet carefully. "It doesn't look right," she said. "There's something about the diamonds—they don't have that beautiful hint of blue anymore."

She glanced up at Brenda and saw the look of consternation and fear that came over her face. What's the matter with her? Lady Em asked herself, then looked back at the bracelet. It's not the one Richard gave me, she thought. I know it isn't. I haven't worn so much of my jewelry in years, she thought. Is it possible she's been stealing it and substituting it with junk?

In that moment she was sure she was right. Don't let her know that you know, she warned herself. "Well, you can use the polishing cloth to brighten it up when you get a chance, Brenda," she said, "and if that doesn't work, I'll have Celia Kilbride give it a deep cleaning when we get home."

Lady Em sighed. "I've had enough of playing with my jewelry. I think I'll rest for a bit. I've asked Roger to stop by at eleven o'clock. I want to have a private chat with him. Why don't you take some time for yourself?"

32

After the ceremony with Devon Michaelson, Celia half-willingly agreed to join Alvirah and Willy for lunch in the buffet dining room. "I read that you can get everything from sushi to Chinese food to Central European," Alvirah told her.

They would meet at one o'clock in the restaurant, and beforehand she took a long walk around the promenade deck.

When she returned to her stateroom, she showered, dressed in blue slacks and a blue-and-white top, ordered breakfast and went over her notes for her lectures. Today she would talk about other fabled jewels through the ages and the histories of individual pieces of jewelry that had been given in love, appeasement or as a bribe.

One of the stories was about the elegant wife of William Randolph Hearst, who discovered that her husband had built San Simeon castle for his mistress, the actress Marion Davies. Celia went over what she would say in her head.

" 'When he was beginning the newspaper business, I was there, and I gave him five sons,' " Ms. Hearst was reported to have said to a friend. Then she went to Tiffany's and ordered a magnificent long pearl necklace and told the saleswoman to send the bill to her husband. The story goes that when he got it, he never even mentioned it to her.

"And then a Hearst heiress and her husband were invited to a formal dinner on the *Britannia* when Queen Elizabeth II sailed on her to Los Angeles. Ms. Hearst was wearing the family emeralds.

"When she boarded the *Britannia*, the Queen was wearing her own magnificent emeralds. Ms. Hearst confided to a friend, 'Compared to hers, mine looked as if they came out of a Cracker Jack box!' "

The final personal story would be about the King of Saudi Arabia who was accompanied by his daughter to a White House state dinner. The twenty-two-year-old princess kept the President waiting twenty minutes, an unpardonable breach of etiquette. But that fact was forgotten by the media, whose focus was on her three-strand necklace, a stunning mixture of priceless gemstones from diamonds and rubies to emeralds and sapphires.

It's human to enjoy the gossipy stories, Celia thought, and telling just a few never failed to spice up a lecture.

Satisfied that she was prepared for the presentation, Celia looked at her watch. It was quarter of one and time to join Alvirah and Willy in the buffet dining room for lunch. It's hardly self-service, she thought, remembering other luxurious ocean liners she had been on that had the same kind of service. When a passenger had finished making a selection, a waiter was always there to carry the tray to a table and serve whatever beverage was requested.

She looked at her watch again and decided she had enough time to call her lawyer. She wanted to see if he had heard anything about whether they might be viewing her differently after the *People* magazine article. Randolph Knowles was not in his office. His secretary promised he would return the call. Celia could not help asking, "Any word from the US Attorney's Office?"

"No, nothing. Oh, wait a minute. Mr. Knowles just walked in." Celia heard her say, "Ms. Kilbride is on the phone." Then, when Randolph said, "Hello, Celia," she knew she was not going to hear good news. She did not go through the formality of greeting him. "What's going on, Randolph?" she asked.

"Celia, it's not good," Randolph told her. "Your ex-fiancé is such a convincing liar that the US Attorney's Office just called me to say that they may ask the FBI to interview you again when you get home."

Celia thought numbly, I'm flying back from London the day we dock in Southampton. That's only a few days from now. She remembered the stony faces of the FBI agents who had interrogated her.

Randolph was talking. "Celia, they put you through the mill already and they believed you. This is simply another hurdle." But it was obvious from his tone that he was not convinced.

"I hope it is." Celia pressed the red button on her cell phone. If only I hadn't promised the Meehans I would join them, she thought passionately. But she had, and a few minutes later a waiter was pulling out a chair for her at the table where they were sitting.

They both smiled and Alvirah greeted her warmly. "Celia, as I said before, we're so happy to be able to have a chance to chat with you. Willy told me he was initially sorry he went into Carruthers to ask about the prices of some of the rings he saw in the display cases, but then you came along and made him feel so comfortable."

What she did not add was that she was dying to talk to Celia about her crooked ex-boyfriend. She was sure that when his trial came up she would be asked to cover it in her column in the *Globe*.

Of course she would not just plunge into that right away. "Why don't we all make our selections," she suggested. "And then we can chat."

But a few minutes later, when Willy was happily enjoying a plate of sushi and she was halfway through a bowl of linguini with clam sauce, she noticed that Celia had eaten only a few bites of her chicken salad.

"Celia, if you don't like the salad, you can get something else," Alvirah said.

Celia felt a sudden lump in her throat and knew her eyes were filling with tears. Quickly she reached in her bag for her sunglasses. But Alvirah had noticed. "Celia," she said in a voice rich with concern, "we know the stress you're under."

"I guess everybody knows. And if they didn't know before, they'll find out today."

"Celia, sadly, what your fiancé did is all too common, but everyone is sorry for you being caught in that mess."

"Everyone except my closest friends, who lost money they couldn't afford to lose and blame me for having introduced Steven to them."

"You lost money too," Willy said.

"Two hundred fifty thousand dollars! In other words, every cent I had," Celia said. Unwillingly, she realized that it was somehow comforting to unburden herself to people who were virtual strangers. But then she remembered that Willy had told her so much about them when she was helping him select the ring. He had explained to her how Alvirah had formed a support group for people who had won the lottery, so they wouldn't be taken in by con men. She knew that she had liked Willy on sight and liked Alvirah the minute Willy described her.

And it was a relief to be able to share her anxiety with people who were looking at her with kind and sympathetic expressions.

The words came tumbling out. "Steven gave an interview to *People* magazine, and in it he said that I was part of the scheme to build up his fund by introducing him to my friends. It's going to be all over the media today. Now, because of the article, it looks like the FBI is going to question me again when I get back to New York."

"You *did* tell the truth," Alvirah said. It was not a question.

"Of course I did."

"And Steven What's-his-name has lied to you and everyone else?"

"Yes."

"Then why wouldn't he lie to *People* magazine as well?"

Celia could feel Alvirah's reassurance begin to lift some of the crushing worry from her shoulders. Not completely. She wasn't going to talk now about the fact that her job at Carruthers was in jeopardy. She knew the chief executive had been upset that one of their employees had been linked to a scam. Now, the more she thought about it, the more certain she was that when she got back to New York she would at the least be put on an unpaid leave of absence. I can't keep up with the rent on my apartment and all the other overhead expenses like insurance and utilities for more than three months, not to mention ongoing legal bills, she thought. And then what? Would any jewelry firm want to hire me?

All this flashed through her mind in an instant, but then she blinked away the tears that had not fallen and forced a smile. "I feel as though I've been to confession."

"Just keep this in mind, Celia." Now Alvirah's voice was firm. "You have absolutely no need of absolution in any way, shape or form. Now, eat your salad. Things will work out fine. I can feel it in my bones."

33

Brenda's suite was on the floor below Lady Em's. It was smaller, but had valet service. When Lady Em decided to have her lunch served in her suite and rest for an hour, Brenda went to the buffet restaurant. Even though she was almost desperate with worry, she still had a hearty appetite. She went to the section that served Chinese food and helped herself to wonton soup, pork fried rice and a dumpling. Then on impulse, she grabbed a fortune cookie. As a waiter carried her tray to a small table by the window, she looked around the dining room. About six tables from the one where she was heading to, she saw Celia with Alvirah and her husband. They seemed to be engrossed in conversation. No idle chatter for *them*, she thought sarcastically.

Her eyes filled with hatred as she looked at Celia. She's the one who could put me in prison, she thought bitterly.

"Here you are, ma'am," the waiter, a handsome Asian man, said as he removed dishes from the tray and placed them on the table.

Brenda did not thank him. He asked if she cared for a beverage. "Regular coffee with cream and sugar." Her tone was dismissive.

What was she going to do? she asked herself. And why now does Lady Em all of a sudden get the idea that her jewelry doesn't look right? For years she's ignored all but the best pieces in her collection. And for years she has been adding to it, buying a ten-thousand-dollar ring or a forty-thousand-dollar bracelet she saw in a store window, as she did on St. Thomas. She wears her new pieces a few times, then tosses them into the master safe in the apartment.

Brenda began sipping the wonton soup and thought of Ralphie. She had met him five years ago, and they had been together ever since. She had not told Lady Em about him, of course. Ralph was a sixty-seven-year-old insurance salesman whom she happily supported in the three-room apartment Lady Em had purchased for her to use, and where Brenda spent her free weekends. Not that there were many of *them*, she thought resentfully. But after she's in bed and with the sleep-in housekeeper in her apartment, I can escape there.

After she told Ralph about Lady Em's incredible jewelry collection, he had asked her how frequently she wore all those pieces. She had told him that Lady Em would often buy a necklace or earrings or a ring or a bracelet that had caught her eye, wear it a few times and then forget all about it or simply not bother to put it on again.

Ralph's next question had been, "Is everything insured?"

The answer was that Lady Em only insured the pieces that were worth over one hundred thousand dollars.

And that's how it began. Ralph had a jeweler friend who worked with them to substitute fake gems for the ones in Lady Em's safe. It was so easy. Brenda had the code to the safe. She would take a piece out and give it to Ralphie. He would bring it to the jeweler, who would create a similar-looking piece. When it was ready, she would put it in the safe. The one piece of jewelry that wasn't in the safe and that she had never seen was the Cleopatra necklace.

Now as she pushed aside the empty soup bowl and began to eat the pork fried rice, Brenda cursed herself for being stupid enough to have fooled with the "picnic" bracelet that Sir Richard had bought for Lady Em when they were strolling down Fifth Avenue. Lady Em cherished it. God knows I heard the story often enough to realize that I should have left it alone, Brenda thought bitterly.

She and Ralphie had over two million dollars thanks to selling Lady Em's jewelry, but what good would it do them if Lady Em had that bracelet checked by Celia Kilbride, let alone all the others that had been switched? She would prosecute them, that was for sure. She had once done it to a chef who had been padding the food bills. "I pay you very well," she told him. "Now *you* will pay for your greed."

Brenda finished everything on her plate and went to the dessert section. She selected a generous slice of chocolate layer cake and returned to the table. It had already been cleared except for the coffee cup, which had been refilled.

I like traveling like this, she thought. At least I did until I met Ralphie and fell in love. I have to say these twenty years with Lady Em have been interesting, the trips all around the world, the Broadway plays, the people I've met.

When they got back to New York next Thursday, it would be the beginning of the end—and fast. But if something happened to Lady Em before then, there would be no worries, and the three hundred thousand Lady Em planned to leave her in her will would be hers.

Brenda opened her fortune cookie. *Big changes in your life are coming. Be ready.* Well, that could be really good or really bad, she thought, as she crumpled the slip of paper and dropped it.

She glanced at the table where Celia Kilbride and the Meehans were pushing back their chairs. A sudden thought hit her. Would Lady Em be troubled enough about the bracelet to give it to Celia to examine *before* they were back in New York? If she did, would Celia be able to tell that it would never have been displayed in the window of Harry Winston? Of course, she would.

It was another frightening possibility.

34

Roger had come back from his meeting with Lady Em with his worry confirmed. She had introduced the subject gently. "Roger, you know how grateful I am to you for the way you have handled my affairs, but I am very old and have heart trouble. As you know, virtually all of my money will go to the charities I have always supported. If there are any discrepancies in what I have, or where it came from, I want to be around to help tidy them up. That's why, although I trust you and the work you have done, I think it would be a good idea to have an outside accounting firm go over everything and be sure my affairs are completely in order."

Lady Em had waved off Roger's initial protest by saying that she did not want to be late for her hair appointment.

Two hours later Yvonne and Roger were the first two at their table for the luncheon service in the formal dining room. They had gone there in the hope of talking to Lady Em. They would try to dissuade her from spending a great deal of money for an unnecessary review of her finances.

Roger had spent a near-sleepless night planning how to deal with the subject if Lady Em brought it up at the meeting.

When given the opportunity, Roger would point out to Lady Em that all the charities would have their own legal counsel carefully examine the terms of her will and her holdings. At this age, why would she trouble herself? His chief argument would be that in all the years the IRS had reviewed her income tax returns, they had never once ordered an audit. "And believe me, Lady Em," he would say, "they go over your returns with a fine-tooth comb."

The prospect of persuading her to not go forward with the review became so likely in his mind that he actually began to feel better. As he and Yvonne sat at the table waiting for Lady Em, he did get in a word of warning to his wife. "And stop looking so damn bored. You're not that interesting yourself, you know."

"Look who's talking," Yvonne snapped, but she did force an amiable expression onto her face. After fifteen minutes passed, they knew that they would be dining alone and ordered lunch. Just as it was being served, Professor Henry Longworth came into the dining room and joined them.

"We haven't had much chance to chat," he said with a smile. "So it will be nice to visit with the two of you alone."

Roger returned the sentiment while Yvonne asked herself if the professor was going to start talking about Shakespeare. She had tolerated yesterday's lecture but had no intention of going to his next one. She had little interest in making small talk with him.

Her mind quickly returned to the abiding worry that if Lady Em commissioned an outside review of her finances, Roger would go to prison. She had absolutely no faith in Roger's ability to change Lady Em's mind.

She began to consider her own options. Divorce Roger before the inevitable scandal broke? That might help keep her out of legal trouble, but if he were found to be an embezzler, they'd probably claw back most of the money in their accounts.

Another possibility occurred to her: Roger has a five-million-dollar term life insurance policy, and I am the sole beneficiary. If anything happened to him, I would get the money.

And he does like to sit on the rail of our balcony even when the ocean is choppy.

35

Celia's second lecture was even more widely attended than the first one. She smiled when she saw Lady Em sitting next to Alvirah and Willy in the first row. Alvirah was chatting away with Lady Em, and Celia was sure that by the time she began speaking Alvirah would be Lady Em's new friend. As she walked to the lectern, everyone fell silent, but before she spoke, she glanced at Alvirah, who gave her an encouraging smile.

My new best friend, she thought.

After thanking everyone for attending, Celia began. "Emeralds came into usage as jewelry not long after gold. Emerald derives its name from the Ancient Greek word for green. The first known emerald mines were in Egypt. Researchers have dated these mines from 330 B.C. and they were still being worked as late as the 1700s. Cleopatra was reported to have favored emeralds above all other stones."

She spoke about the emerald's curative powers and the use of emeralds by early physicians who believed that the best method for restoring the eyes was by looking at an emerald. Its soft green comfort would remove weariness and strain. Truth be told, they were onto something. Even today the color green is recognized to reduce stress and be soothing to the eye.

Wearing an emerald was believed to reveal the truth, or lack of it, in a lover's oath. It was also purported to make one an eloquent speaker. Placing her hand on her pendant and pushing it forward from her blouse, Celia said, "I don't own one, so I can't put that theory to the test today." Wide laughter from the audience followed.

She then talked about other jewels that had belonged to pharaohs and kings and had been used as ransom, or to pay debts, and other precious stones that were rumored to have curative powers.

When she was finished with the question-and-answer session, one of the guests observed, "Ms. Kilbride, you made us all want to have more jewelry, or wear what we do have every day."

"Sadly, many people keep lovely jewelry in a safe deposit box and never wear it," Celia replied. "Of course you have to be careful with it, but why not enjoy it?"

The luncheon with Alvirah and Willy, and the obvious success of the lecture, which was roundly applauded, gave Celia a temporary lift. She returned to her suite. Her long walk on the deck and early morning awakening had left her feeling tired, so she decided to nap before she prepared for the Captain's cocktail party and the dinner following it.

And that, of course, was another reminder. The expensive gown that she would be wearing she had bought for the honeymoon which, thankfully, never happened.

I might as well take my own advice and enjoy it, she thought. It will be a long, cold day before I spend money like that again.

36

Devon Michaelson wondered if he had made a mistake inviting the other guests at his table to the service this morning. He knew that his startled reaction when the chaplain, Father Baker, offered to pray over the urn had been noticed by Alvirah Meehan, and perhaps by others in the small group. His hope was that they might think he was an atheist.

In fact, he had been raised in a devout Catholic family. Even though he had fallen away from any practice of religion, he had imagined the horror his mother would have felt if he let a priest say a prayer over cigar ashes.

I can't let anyone start wondering about me, he thought. And by now I should know that I have never been given the luxury of making mistakes.

Yvonne, Dana and Valerie were finishing their second glasses of wine. They had spent the late morning and early afternoon sunbathing by the pool. As they were talking, Valerie was scanning the list of activities.

"Listen to this," Yvonne interrupted. "There's going to be a lecture about the Hamptons including the story of a real-life witch from East Hampton."

"I know who that must be," Dana offered. "It's Julie Winston, the former model who just married the chairman of Browning Brothers. I got stuck seated next to her at a charity ball and—"

"If we're talking witches, it's got to be Ethel Pruner. Seven of us were on a committee with her to organize flower arrangements and we all wanted to quit after the first meeting—"

Valerie held up both hands and laughed. "I think they're referring to a witch that lived in the 1600s. It starts in fifteen minutes. What do you say?"

"Let's go," Dana and Yvonne said in unison as they all stood up.

The presenter introduced himself as Charles Dillingham Chadwick. He was a slender man in his mid-forties, bald, and of average height. Chadwick had that trademark Hamptons ability to speak without moving his lower jaw, but at the same time he had a twinkle in his eye and a willingness to poke fun at himself.

"Thank you all so very much for coming. One of my earliest happy childhood memories is of my father explaining how our family traces its ancestry all the way back to the *Mayflower* and how our ancestors once owned a considerable amount of land in what is now the Hamptons. My foremost unhappy childhood memory is when I learned that they sold their land for a pittance one hundred years ago."

Wide laughter followed. Dana said to Valerie and Yvonne, "This is going to be more fun than we thought."

Chadwick cleared his throat and continued. "I hope you will find as fascinating as I do how a sleepy collection of farming and fishing villages on the easternmost tip of Long Island emerged into one of the world's foremost playgrounds for the rich and famous. But let's begin with a story of a neighborly dispute which almost resulted in one of the Hamptons' early settlers being, shall we say, barbequed.

"In the early days of the Hamptons the Puritans held sway. Thirty-five years before the infamous witch trials in Salem, Massachusetts, Easthampton had its own 'bewitching' experience.

"In February 1658, shortly after giving birth, sixteen-year-old Elizabeth Gardiner became very ill and began ranting about being the victim of witchcraft. Young Gardiner would die a day later, but not before she identified her neighbor Goody Garlick as her tormentor. Poor Goody had been the target of other unsavory accusations. She was viewed as the culprit when livestock mysteriously died.

"A review of the Hamptons court records of the time reveals that people were constantly accusing, arguing with and suing each other over the most trivial of matters—I'm tempted to add that little has changed to this very day. Poor Goodie, it appears, was headed for a nasty experience.

"But Garlick was the recipient of some, shall we say, Goody luck, when the East Hampton magistrates, unable to make a decision, referred her case to a higher court in Hartford, the colony that owned the Hamptons at that time.

"Her case was heard by Governor John Winthrop, Jr. Winthrop was a scholar who believed that the magical forces of nature were more responsible for events than people. There may have been a bit of snobbery at work. He was skeptical that a farmer's wife with little education could perform magical acts. A verdict of not guilty was rendered along with some judicial advice for the cantankerous Hamptons residents. I quote, 'It is desired and expected by this court that you should carry neighborly and peaceably without offense to Mr. Garlick and his wife, and that they should do like to you.'

"Is this little anecdote important? I think so. After Winthrop's decision, Easthampton had no more accusations of witchcraft, while that subject would paralyze communities in Massachusetts for years to come. As for Hamptons residents behaving neighborly, that remains a work in progress."

37

The Captain's cocktail party was held in his large, beautifully decorated suite. Soft blues and pale greens on the walls and furnishings were the color scheme. Smiling waiters offered drinks and hors d'oeuvres. Celia had fastened back her dark hair with a gold clip and let it cascade down on her shoulders. Her moss-green gown was shimmering chiffon. The earrings that had been her mother's were her only jewelry.

She did not realize it, but the eyes of the Captain, as well as most of the other men present, lingered on her as she chatted with other guests. Lady Em arrived shortly after her. She was wearing a simple black gown which set off the breathtaking three-strand emerald necklace that had once adorned Cleopatra, Queen of Egypt, and had not been seen in public in one hundred years. Startling in its beauty, each emerald sparkled in unblemished clarity. Lady Em's white hair was piled softly on her head; her wide hazel eyes and long lashes gave hints of the beauty she had been, and her straight carriage combined to present a regal, commanding image. Her earrings were pear-shaped diamonds, and other than that she wore only her diamond wedding band, to ensure that nothing would distract from the awe-inspiring necklace.

Like Celia, she had decided to put aside her concerns for the evening. She wanted to enjoy the sensation that she knew she was causing. It reminded her of those faraway days when she bowed to the thunderous applause of packed theaters as a prima ballerina.

And although he was always present in her subconscious mind, it so vividly brought back memories of Richard, including when he was waiting at the stage door that wonderful night in London when they first met. Handsome, courtly Richard, who had stepped forward from the crowd of admirers, reached for her hand and kissed it.

And never let it go, she thought wistfully, as she accepted a glass of wine.

Alvirah was wearing the beige gown and matching jacket that Willy liked best. In the late afternoon she had had her hair done at the beauty salon and even allowed herself to be persuaded to have light makeup applied to her face.

As always, Captain Fairfax was an impeccable host. The intense worry he was harboring did not show in his face or manner. He had three concerns: the Man with One Thousand Faces might be in this room right now salivating for Lady Haywood's emeralds, the sea was already beginning to show a trace of the heavy storm they were sailing into, and the engine problem had already put them behind schedule.

Ted Cavanaugh, the partner in a law firm, was the next guest to come over to him. Fairfax had been made aware of his background. Son of the former ambassador to Egypt and the Court of Saint James, celebrated for seeking to reclaim stolen antiquities. The Captain had a twenty-three-year-old daughter. This is the kind of chap I wish Lisa would bring home, he thought. Good-looking, successful, impeccable family background, instead of that long-haired musician, a harmonica player.

He extended his hand to Ted. "Welcome, Mr. Cavanaugh. I hope you have been enjoying your cruise."

"Indeed I have been," Ted replied while returning the Captain's firm handshake.

Fairfax smiled.

His attention was diverted by the arrival of Devon Michaelson, the Interpol agent whose cover was a retired engineer. The Captain moved across the room to greet him but was blocked by Anna DeMille's swift rush to Michaelson's side. Instead he turned to the couple on his left. He had been briefed on them. The Meehans had won forty million dollars in the lottery about five years ago, and Mrs. Meehan had gained prominence as a newspaper columnist who also managed to solve crimes.

"Mr. and Mrs. Meehan," he said with the pleasant smile that always masked his true concerns.

"Alvirah and Willy," Alvirah said promptly. "Captain, it's such a privilege to be on the maiden voyage of this beautiful ship. It will always be a wonderful memory for us."

At that moment the door was pushed open and Yvonne Pearson burst in. "My husband fell overboard!" she shrieked. "My husband fell overboard!"

38

"Come with me" had been Captain Fairfax's response to an emotionally wrought Yvonne. He led her out of the crowded lounge to a private room. As they walked, he barked orders into his phone instructing John Saunders, his chief of security, to meet him at the purser's desk. It was only when the door to the small office was closed behind him that he and Saunders began to interview Yvonne.

"Mrs. Pearson," Fairfax began, "tell me precisely what you saw and heard in regard to what happened to your husband."

Yvonne spoke haltingly, trying to choke back sobs. "We, I mean Roger and I, were in our suite. We were talking out on the balcony. We had both had a few drinks. Roger was sitting up on the railing. I asked him to not do that. He told me to mind my own business. And then he fell." Yvonne buried her head in her hands and sobbed.

"Mrs. Pearson," the Captain began, "I know how upsetting this is for you, and I'm sorry to have to ask you all these questions. I guarantee you we want to find your husband just as much as you do. But before I consider turning this ship around and going back to try to find him, I have to know exactly what you saw."

Yvonne wiped tears away and accepted the tissue offered by Saunders. Between sniffles a thought occurred to her. She had immediately raced to the cocktail lounge to announce that Roger had gone overboard. She was desperately worried that she should have waited longer. She had no idea how long it would take for the ship to turn around and go back. Or would they quickly send a small boat back to look for him? But the Captain doesn't seem to be in a hurry to begin the search, she thought.

"I'm sorry. This is so upsetting. I have to admit I was upset when Roger told me to mind my own business. I went back in the suite and I angrily slid the balcony door shut behind me. A minute later when I went back out to tell him it was time to head over to the cocktail party, he was gone." She burst into tears again, then considered swooning, perhaps even a full-blown faint, but she wasn't certain it would appear genuine.

It was Saunders who asked the next question, while holding out another tissue. "Mrs. Pearson, you said, 'a minute later,' you went out to the balcony and your husband was gone. The reason we are questioning you so closely is that most reports of a person going overboard turn out to be false alarms. The missing person is almost always located somewhere else on the ship, sometimes unfortunately in a place he shouldn't be. What precisely did you do in that minute between when you last saw your husband on the balcony sitting on the deck rail and when you went back to get him to go to the cocktail party?"

Yvonne made a conscious effort to hide an immense wave of relief that was washing over her. "I did go into the bathroom for just a moment."

"Did you close the door when you went to the bathroom?" Saunders asked.

"Of course I did."

"So you were in the bathroom for at least a minute with the door closed," the Captain said. "And is it possible that your husband could have left the suite while you," he hesitated, "had the door closed?"

"Well, I certainly think I would have heard the balcony door and then the suite door open and close," she said. "But, you know, the flush noise is a little on the loud side."

"It is, and I apologize for that," the Captain said. "But if I slow this ship down or turn it around, we would lose the opportunity to reach Southampton on time. This would be a major disruption for our guests, many of whom are heading straight to the airports for scheduled flights. I recommend that we conduct a thorough search of the ship to try to find your husband. If we are not successful, we will then consider what to do next."

Saunders reached forward and handed Yvonne a sheet of paper and a pen. "Mrs. Pearson. There is a protocol that we follow in these unfortunate situations. I am going to ask you to complete this form that will include your written account of what happened in your suite around the time you last saw your husband. When you are finished and you have reviewed it for accuracy, you and I will both sign the form."

Yvonne was feeling absolutely buoyant. "I so appreciate that we are all doing everything we can to find my poor dear Roger."

39

Yvonne had refused Captain Fairfax's offer to have one of his men accompany her back to her cabin. "I'll be all right," she had said. "I just need some time alone to pray for my dear Roger."

After she left, the Captain asked Saunders, "What do you think?"

"She admitted she didn't see him fall overboard. She also admitted that they both had a lot to drink. And this was before they were planning to go to your cocktail party. I'm not at all convinced that he went overboard."

"Neither am I," Fairfax agreed. "The last time I had an incident like this on a ship I commanded, the wife insisted she saw her husband get washed over when the ship hit a swell. If the chap did go over, he got very lucky. He landed unharmed in the bed of a floozy passenger several levels below."

"So, what are we going to do?" Saunders asked.

Before the Captain could answer, his phone rang. He picked it up. Even without the phone on speaker mode, Saunders could hear every word coming from the mouth of Gregory Morrison, the blustery ship owner.

"What the hell is going on?" asked the voice on the other end of the phone.

"A report has been made by a woman passenger that her husband may have—"

"I know that, dammit," Morrison bellowed. "I want to know what in hell you're doing about it."

"Mr. Saunders and I have questioned the wi—" The Captain had started to say "widow" but caught himself. "The wife of the man who may have gone overboard. Both she and her husband had been drinking a lot, and she admits she didn't actually see him go over. My recommendation is—"

"I'll tell you what we are not going to do, Fairfax. Under no circumstances are you to turn this ship around. I don't want to hear word one about a Williamson turn."

The Captain rubbed his temples as he held the phone. A Williamson turn or maneuver is where the ship is turned around at a high rate of speed. Like all captains, he had been trained on this. If he were convinced that Pearson had truly gone over the side, he would order the Williamson turn and direct crewmen to deploy high-power spotlights shined on the water. The special rescue boats with outboard motors would be put in the water. It was within his discretion to also send lifeboats to aid in the search. His SQM, *Safety and Quality Manual*, laid out the procedure he should follow.

But he was compelled to act only if an eyewitness, or preferably two, saw the passenger go over the side. In this case he had a boozy eyewitness who, after a little probing, admitted that she did not see her husband go overboard. And he had an owner who was going to fight him every step of the way if he took aggressive measures to look for Pearson in the water.

"I am going to order that the ship be thoroughly searched. We have the passport photos of all the passengers. I'll direct that copies of Pearson's picture be made and distributed to the crewmen who will undertake the search."

"Okay," Morrison said, sounding mollified. "But I don't want the passengers ordered back to their rooms. Let the crewmen bang on the cabin doors asking for Pearson. If he's in one of the rooms, he'll answer."

The call ended before Fairfax could respond.

It was Saunders who spoke first. "For the second time I'll ask, what are we going to do?"

"You heard the man," the Captain said. "We're going to search the ship."

40

Lady Em, Brenda and Celia sat together offering silent prayers that Roger would be saved, even while they realized there was almost no hope that if he had gone overboard, he had managed to stay afloat in the treacherous waters.

Fairfax's voice came over the ship's public address system. "This is your captain. We are trying to locate a Mr. Roger Pearson. Mr. Pearson, if you can hear this message, would you please contact the bridge. If any passenger has seen Mr. Pearson in the last twenty minutes, would you please call the bridge. That is all. Thank you."

Celia spoke first. "I wonder if that's standard procedure, to first search the ship for somebody they think might have gone overboard."

Lady Em turned to Brenda. "Go to Yvonne," she said. "She should have someone she knows with her."

"I'm afraid I wouldn't do her much good," she confided to Celia when Brenda had left. Lady Em was wracked with regret and anger. She knew that her announcement that she was having another accounting firm go over her finances may have caused Roger to deliberately go over the railing. She had not seen him at lunch, but had run into him when she took a brief walk on the deck at five o'clock. With nervous energy, he had launched into explaining why she should not waste money on such an unnecessary expense. She had finally stopped him by saying, "I don't want to discuss it. I hope

I have made my decision perfectly clear. And frankly, it concerns me that you are so adamantly against it."

They were the last words she had uttered to Roger. Did he fall, or did I drive him to suicide? she wondered.

Twenty minutes later, as a member of the crew went from one group of passengers to the other urging them to please enjoy dinner, she reluctantly picked up the menu.

"I would suggest that we all need a strong drink," Professor Long-worth volunteered.

"I think that's a very good idea," Celia said fervently, as she noted how very ill Lady Em suddenly looked. And very old, she thought. She's so commanding and energetic that we forget her age. And, of course, Roger has been a close friend as well as working for her all these years.

They were silent at dinner, each busy with his or her own thoughts.

41

The table where Alvirah and Willy were sitting had had the same reaction as that of their neighbors. Willy had even insisted that Alvirah join him in having a vodka martini. Devon Michaelson, Ted Cavanaugh and Anna DeMille were of the same mind. Anna was the one who voiced the mutual sentiment. "It's hard to think that last night at this time the poor man was sitting only a few feet away from us."

After hearing the Captain's announcement about the search for Roger, they were confused about what to think. Ted volunteered, "For whatever reason, there must be some doubt about his wife's story that he fell overboard."

Alvirah's reaction was remembering the quarrel she and Willy had overheard outside their suite last night between Roger and Yvonne. She wondered if that was only a temporary flare-up. Did Roger's admission to Yvonne that he was facing twenty years in prison drive him to deliberately go overboard? She was sure Willy was thinking the same thing, but, of course, he wouldn't say it.

Anna DeMille secretly wished that Roger had waited until later to fall overboard. She had been enjoying the Captain's party. There had been at least a dozen A-list celebrities there. She had left Devon's side and drifted over to the rap star Bee Buzz and his wife Tiffany. They had both been very cordial and laughed when she told them her story about not being related to Cecil B. DeMille. That was so unlike the time they turned their backs on her when she tried to start a conversation on the deck. Then, as they all sat down to hear the latest news about Roger Pearson, she had stumbled and Devon Michaelson had put his arm around her to save her from falling. It had felt so good. She had hoped he would never let her go. Later she pretended to stumble again, but this time he didn't seem to notice. She looked around.

"And now to think, we're all still dressed up for a party," she said unnecessarily. "It makes you wonder, doesn't it?"

"We never know from one minute to the next, do we?" Alvirah agreed.

Neither Devon nor Ted Cavanaugh bothered to answer her, each busy with his own troubled thoughts.

42

Miles away from the now-vanished ship, Roger Pearson was trying desperately to keep a slow, steady pace as he tread water. Think rationally, he told himself. I'm a very strong swimmer. If I can keep moving, I may have a chance.

He gulped in air as he continued to swim. This is a busy travel lane, he told himself. Another ship may come along. I've got to make it. Even if I end up in prison, I don't care. She pushed me over. *She pushed me over.* She'll go to prison too. And if they don't believe me, there's one other thing I can do. I can cancel that five-million-dollar policy. That's probably why she tried to kill me. Well, I'll fight her with every ounce of strength I have. I need to live to cancel that policy.

Roger then remembered the survival training course he had taken when he was a sixteen-year-old Boy Scout. It had worked in the swimming pool. Could he do it now when it might save his life?

Holding his breath, Roger let himself slip under the water as he struggled to wriggle out of his trousers. Kicking hard to keep afloat, he managed to tie the ends of his pants legs into a double knot. Then he looped the pants over his head with the knot behind his neck. The next, most difficult move was to scoop air and water through the open waistband of the trousers, then hold and twist the waistband to trap the air.

A feeling of real hope washed over him when the air inside the pants formed a pillow that floated about six inches above the water. To test his makeshift flotation device, he stopped kicking and held still. With no effort on his part he was now buoyant in his improvised life jacket.

Although he knew that air would slowly escape and he would have to repeat the process, he was sure he had increased the length of time he could stay afloat without succumbing to exhaustion. Would it be long enough?

A wave washed over him, causing his eyes to fill with salt spray, but he closed them and persevered.

43

It had been necessary to stop Roger from being arrested. After a late afternoon walk on the deck, he had come back to the suite pale and sweaty. "It's no use," he had said. "I've tried to talk her out of doing an outside audit of her finances, but all I did was make her more suspicious."

Now that it was done, Yvonne was filled with dread. Roger had sat on the rail for only a few minutes, then said, "Too choppy for this perch." Just as he tried to move forward, he almost lost his balance. That was when she lunged forward and pushed him with all her might.

Before he fell, his look had been one of surprise. Then as his body began to go down, he screamed, "No, no, no . . ." Her last sight of him was watching his legs and feet go over the rail.

She knew she should have waited longer before telling anyone that he had fallen overboard. It seemed like only minutes before the Captain and other personnel began to search the ship looking for him.

It was only then that she remembered that Roger was a strong swimmer and that he had been on the swim team in college. Suppose they found him alive? There was no way that she could make him believe that she had accidentally pushed him when she meant to help him down off the railing.

The consequences for her of Roger being rescued were so over-powering that she was trembling and shaking when the doctor gave her a tranquilizer. Brenda offered to wrap a blanket around her as she sat on the sofa in the living room of the suite.

It was time to get rid of Brenda, who with uncharacteristic sympathy had also offered to sleep on the couch.

As Brenda was holding the blanket, they could hear a loud knock on the door across the hall. A young crewmember yelled through the door. "Excuse me. We are looking for a Mr. Roger Pearson. Is he in this room?"

They heard a faint "no" from the room's occupant. "Thank you," the crewmember said as he moved to the next door.

Brenda turned to Yvonne. "Am I helping you by being with you or would you rather be alone?"

"Oh, thank you, I guess I'll be all right alone. I may have to get used to being on my own. But thank you again, and I will be all right."

When Brenda was finally gone, Yvonne got up and poured a stiff scotch on the rocks. She tilted the glass in a silent tribute to Roger. You'd have committed suicide before you faced twenty years in prison, she thought. She wondered how soon she would be getting the five million dollars in insurance money. Probably within a week after she was back in New York. If Roger did siphon off a lot of money from Lady Em, where was it? Did he have secret bank accounts he hadn't told her about? Well, one thing for sure. If she were ever questioned by the FBI, she was sure that she could convince them that she knew nothing about Roger's finances.

With that comforting thought the self-made widow decided to treat herself to a second, generous serving of Chivas Regal scotch.

44

"Come in," Fairfax said after Security Chief Saunders knocked on his door.

"Did you find anything?"

"Nothing, Captain. No one reported seeing him over the last two hours. I am confident that he is not on the ship."

"Which means he probably went overboard at the time his wife said he did."

"I'm afraid so, sir."

Fairfax paused. "The Pearsons were in a cabin on the ultra deck. Is that correct?"

"Yes."

"So that means when he hit the water he had fallen at least sixty feet. What do you think about his chances of survival?"

"Slim to none, sir. He fell over backwards and he had been drinking. If he survived the fall, he likely would have been knocked unconscious. If that were the case, he would have sunk quickly, especially when you consider how heavy his wet clothes would have been. Even if we had gone back for him immediately, Captain, I don't believe the outcome would have been different."

"I know, and I agree," the Captain sighed. "I'll call Morrison and fill him in. I want you to call Chaplain Baker and tell him to come and meet me here."

"Very good, sir," Saunders said as he headed to the door.

Morrison picked up on the first ring. After explaining how they reached the conclusion that Pearson had to be dead, the Captain told the owner that he and the Chaplain were going over to talk to Pearson's wife.

The owner's voice rose to a bellow. "I know the two of you will do a wonderful job breaking the bad news to the woman. Say whatever you have to say to calm her down, but under *no* circumstances are we going back to look for him."

45

It seemed as though nobody wanted to go to bed. Although the evening entertainment, a duo performing songs from prominent operas, had been canceled, the bars with tables and chairs were nearly filled. The casino was even more crowded than usual.

Trying to escape her thoughts, Lady Em had invited her tablemates to have a nightcap with her. That was where Brenda found them after Yvonne told her to leave. Everyone asked how Yvonne was faring.

As Brenda was answering, word began to circulate around the room that the search for Roger had not been successful. The Captain and Chaplain Baker had gone to Yvonne's room to tell her that because Roger was almost certainly dead, the ship was not going to undertake a search and rescue effort.

Walking ahead of his group, Ted Cavanaugh had selected a table for four. Alvirah and Willy were with him, and Alvirah did not miss the fact that Ted had rushed to grab a nearby table as soon as he spotted where Lady Em was seated. Nor did she miss the fact that Lady Em caught his eye and abruptly turned away. Devon Michaelson had again declined to join them. Anna DeMille had grabbed a chair at the bar next to a man her age who appeared to be alone.

Then Lady Em stood up abruptly. "Brenda will sign the check

for me," she said. It was an effort to keep her voice level. "I am very tired. I will say good night to all of you."

Brenda sprang to her feet. "I will accompany you."

God forbid, you thief, Lady Em thought, but her answer was simple and final. "No, that won't be necessary."

There was a nagging pain from her left shoulder going down her arm. She needed to get to her room and take a nitroglycerine pill now.

As she left, she passed by Ted Cavanaugh's chair, hesitated, then continued on.

Alvirah quickly noticed the grim expression on Lady Em's face. She seems upset at him. I wonder why.

A few minutes later, when everyone began to leave, she managed to get in a word with Celia. "I never did get a chance at the Captain's party to tell you that you look so beautiful tonight. How are you doing?"

"About the same," Celia admitted, then added, "Keep feeling in your bones that it will all work out."

Ted Cavanaugh had caught the exchange, puzzled for a minute, then realized why she seemed familiar. Celia Kilbride was the girlfriend of Steven Thorne, the hedge fund swindler. A lot of people think she was in on it, he thought. I wonder if she was. God knows, he thought, she has the face of an angel.

46

The Man with One Thousand Faces did not waste time mourning the loss of Roger Pearson. If anything, he welcomed the distraction it had caused. People were talking about it, mulling it over, saying what a shame that it had happened. They were agreeing that it was not only the personal loss of Roger for his family and friends, but it was also an unfortunate incident for the Castle Line. The maiden voyage of *Queen Charlotte* would be forever remembered as much for the tragedy as for the luxurious experience it offered.

Too bad, he thought, as he felt the swift rush of energy that had always filled him when he was about to pounce. Most times he was able to have the object of his longing without the unfortunate need to take a life to achieve his goal. He knew that might not be the case tonight. It was unlikely that Lady Em would sleep through his visit to her bedroom. He had overheard her lamenting the fact that she was a light sleeper and that any sound could wake her up.

But he could not wait any longer. At the cocktail party he had heard the Captain urging Lady Em to give the necklace into his keeping. If she were to do that, he might never have the chance to steal it again.

At the Captain's party it had been difficult to force his eyes away from it. It was beyond exquisite. It was flawless.

And in a few hours, one way or the other, it would be in his hands.

47

Alvirah and Willy were barely in their suite when she asked in a worried tone, "Willy, did you notice how Lady Em started toward Ted Cavanaugh, then apparently changed her mind?"

"I thought she was just saying good night," Willy said. "What was wrong with that?"

"There's something about the way he stalks Lady Em," Alvirah said firmly.

"What's that supposed to mean, honey?"

"Trust me, he does. Tonight at the cocktail party he went straight over to Lady Em and stared at her necklace. I heard him say, 'That's the most stunning piece of ancient Egyptian jewelry I have ever seen.'"

"That sounds like a nice compliment." Willy yawned in what he hoped would be a signal to Alvirah that he was ready for bed. But if she noticed, it did not deter her need to talk things over.

"Willy, I was walking on the promenade deck this afternoon when you went back to doing the puzzle. Lady Em was about twenty feet ahead of me. Then somebody hurried past me. It was Ted Cavanaugh. He went right up to Lady Em and began to talk to her. Now you know that most people who take a walk on the deck aren't looking to start a conversation with someone they hardly know, especially someone like Lady Em."

"Lady Em isn't the kind you try to get buddy-buddy with," Willy agreed.

"I am absolutely sure that he started to argue with her, because at one of the doors she turned and kind of hurried over to it as if to get away from him."

"Well, before she did that, I bet she put him in his place," Willy said as he stood up and took off his tuxedo jacket. "Honey, it's been quite a day. Why don't we—"

"There's one more thing I noticed," Alvirah interrupted, as she smoothed the crease in the skirt of her evening gown. "We had a pretty good spot to observe what was going on at Lady Em's table last night, and I was kind of looking over because she fascinates me. But then I started to pay attention to Roger and Yvonne.

"Willy, the looks those two exchanged would have stopped a clock. Especially on Yvonne's face. She had such a nasty expression when she stared at him. I just wonder how she's feeling now, after that terrible accident. I mean, how would you feel if we were on the outs and I fell overboard?"

"Honey, we're never on the outs so I wouldn't worry about that too much."

"I suppose not, but still I can't help thinking Yvonne must be so sorry if she and Roger were quarreling before the accident."

She was not sleepy and longed to continue the conversation, but after watching Willy yawn again, she decided to leave it for morning. Then after she was in bed she could not fall asleep. Her bones were telling her that trouble was on the way.

Serious trouble.

48

Brenda knew that Lady Em's quiet dismissal of her when she offered to escort her to her room was one more indication that her employer was aware of the substitution of her jewelry. She was sure of what would happen when Lady Em's suspicion was confirmed.

In her stateroom Brenda remembered in vivid detail when Gerard, the chef of eighteen years, had begged Lady Em not to prosecute him when his theft was discovered. Lady Em told him that a prison term would be good for him. She had said, "I paid to send your three children to good colleges. I remembered their birthdays. I trusted you. Now get out. I'll see you in court."

That's exactly what she'll say to me, Brenda thought frantically. I can't let it happen. She had almost gotten over her attacks of claustrophobia but now had the frightening sensation of a prison door being slammed behind her as she was pushed into a cell.

There was only one way out. Lady Em had admitted at the table that she was not feeling well. If she were to die, her doctor would certainly verify that her heart was in bad shape. She's on a lot of medication. I have a key to her room, Brenda thought. When she goes for a walk, I could go in and mix up some of her pills. Her heart pills are very strong. If I put some of them in all the other vials, they might bring on a heart attack. It was the only possibility that might save me from prison, Brenda thought. Unless I can come up with a better idea.

And maybe I can.

49

After she got rid of Brenda, Yvonne enjoyed her two scotches, then ordered room service. If her butler was surprised by the three-course dinner and the bottle of Pinot Noir the supposedly grieving widow ordered, he did not show it. With an appropriately subdued manner as he served, he reminded her that if she wanted anything at all he would be at her service throughout the night.

She was thankful that the butler had removed the meal cart minutes before the Captain and Chaplain Baker came to speak to her. As she listened to the Captain explain why they would not go back and search for Roger, she was concerned that the scotches might have made her eyes red. But then she relaxed. I'm a grieving widow. My eyes should be red. And if having a few scotches is helping me cope with my tragedy, who would criticize me?

After they left, as she took a last sip, Yvonne started to think of the future. Granted, she would have the five-million-dollar insurance policy, but how long would that last? The Park Avenue apartment and the house in East Hampton were mortgage-free, but they would surely be seized if Roger's theft was discovered. And given the luxurious lifestyle she enjoyed, five million dollars wouldn't go very far.

As she sipped the velvety smooth wine, Yvonne began to consider what options might be available to her. It was clear that Lady Em was going to begin that outside audit as soon as she got home. Was there any way to stop her? After all, the Cleopatra necklace had a curse on it. "Whoever brings this necklace on the sea will not live to reach shore." She smirked when she wondered if Lady Em, like her late husband, enjoyed sitting on the railing of her deck.

For a long time, she continued to mull over possible solutions to her problems. It was easy enough to get rid of Roger.

Would it be easy enough to get rid of Lady Em as well?

50

With a sigh of relief Celia closed the door of her suite and dropped her evening bag on the coffee table. It seemed like such a long time ago that she had shared lunch with Alvirah and Willy and been comforted by Alvirah's cheery optimism that all would be well. She knew that some of the passengers had recognized her as the ex-fiancée and, perhaps, co-conspirator of Steven Thorne. Several times she happened to glance around and catch the embarrassed expression of someone who was looking directly at her.

For long minutes she sat on the edge of the bed trying to tell herself that she must not give up. Now she wondered if it had been a mistake to wear the gown tonight. She had received many compliments on it, but possibly the people who made them had been wondering if it had been bought for her by Steven with other people's money. It might even be possible that some of his investors were on the ship now. He had cut a wide swath with the groups of people who fell for his enticing offer of spectacular returns.

I'm not doing myself any good with this kind of thinking, she told herself as she reached up to take off her earrings. At that moment the phone rang.

The caller did not waste time on a greeting. "Celia, this is Lady Em. This is an outrageous request, but could you possibly come to my suite now? It's very, *very* important. And I know this may sound ridiculous, but would you bring your eyepiece with you?"

Celia could not keep the surprised tone out of her voice as she replied, "If you wish." It was on the tip of her tongue to ask if Lady Em had taken ill, but instead she said, "I'll be right there."

The door of Lady Em's suite was slightly ajar. With a tentative knock Celia pushed it back and stepped into the room. Lady Em was sitting in a large wing chair that was upholstered in red velvet. Celia had the impression of a queen on a throne. There *is* something majestic about Lady Em, she thought. But the old woman's voice was weary as she said, "Thank you, Celia. I had no idea I was going to ask you to make your way here at this hour."

Celia smiled. With quick steps she walked across the room and seated herself in the chair closest to Lady Em. Seeing the obvious fatigue on her face, she did not waste words. "Lady Em, what can I do for you?"

"Celia, before I tell you why I asked you to come over, I want you to know two things. I am aware of the shameful situation regarding your fiancé. I want to assure you that I am one hundred percent certain that you had nothing to do with it."

"Thank you, Lady Em. Hearing you say that is very important to me."

"Celia, it's so good to be able to talk frankly to someone I trust. God knows there are few people in the world I feel I can trust these days. And because of that, I have an overwhelming sense of guilt. I feel very sure that Roger's death was not an accident, but a suicide, and it was because of me."

"Because of you!" Celia exclaimed. "But how could you have any possible reason to think . . . ? "

Lady Em held up her hand. "Celia, listen to me. I can explain very simply. I was at a cocktail party the night before we sailed. Decades ago Richard and I had engaged the accounting and financial management firm that was founded by Roger's grandfather, and we continued the relationship when Roger's father took over. When he died in an accident seven years ago, I stayed with Roger. At the party I saw an old friend who warned me to be very careful. He told me that Roger was not the man of integrity that both his father and grandfather had been. There were rumors that former clients of Roger's believed he had been skimming their accounts. My friend suggested I have my finances checked by an outside firm to be sure that everything was in order.

"I was so troubled by the warning that I told Roger my decision to go forward with an audit." In a voice that was suddenly sad, she said, "I have known Roger since he was a child. When I had my yacht, I frequently invited his mother and father to vacation with me. Of course, they brought Roger along. I joked that he was my surrogate son. Well, some son he turned out to be."

"What would you have done if an audit of your finances proved that you were right?"

"I would have prosecuted him," Lady Em said firmly. "And he knew it. Only a few years ago the chef who had been with me for twenty years and whose children I sent to college began kiting my food and liquor bills. I entertain frequently, and it was many months before I caught on. He was sentenced to two years in prison."

"He deserved that," Celia said firmly. "Anyone who cheats other people, especially those who are good to them, *should* go to prison."

Lady Em paused, then asked, "Celia, did you bring your microscope with you?"

"Yes, I did. It's called a loupe."

For the first time Celia realized that Lady Em was holding a bracelet in her hand.

"Please look at this and tell me what you think of it," she said as she gave it to Celia.

Celia reached into her purse and took out the loupe. Holding it to her eye and rotating the bracelet slowly in front of it, she said, "I'm afraid I don't think very much of it. The diamonds are inferior quality, the kind they use in most of the so-called jewelry bargain centers."

"That is exactly what I expected you to say."

Celia could see the quiver in Lady Em's lip. After a moment Lady Em said, "And, sadly, that means that Brenda, my trusted employee and companion of more than twenty years, has also been stealing from me."

She took the bracelet back. "I will put this in the safe again and act as if nothing's amiss. I'm afraid I've already given Brenda an indication that I am concerned that it didn't seem right."

She reached up and pressed the clasp of the Cleopatra necklace. "Celia, I am desperately worried that I have been a very foolish old woman to have brought this treasure with me on this voyage. I have changed my mind about giving it to the Smithsonian. When I get back to New York, I'm turning it over to my lawyers, and I'll tell them to arrange with Mr. Cavanaugh's firm to have it returned to Egypt."

Celia suspected the answer but still asked, "What made you change your mind?"

"Mr. Cavanaugh is a very nice young man. He made me admit to myself that no matter how much Richard's father paid for the necklace, it had come from a looted tomb. The proper thing to do is return it to Egypt."

"You haven't asked my opinion, Lady Em, but I believe you've made the right decision."

"Thank you, Celia."

Lady Em ran her fingers over the necklace. "This evening at the cocktail party Captain Fairfax begged me to give it to him to put in his personal safe and have a guard outside his cabin to secure it. He said that Interpol has informed him that they believe the Man with One Thousand Faces, an international jewel thief, is on this ship. The Captain urged me to give him the necklace after dinner tonight. I told him I plan to wear it tomorrow night, but I think that might be a mistake."

As the necklace slid from her neck, she caught it and handed it to Celia. "Please take this. Put it in the safe in your room and give it to the Captain in the morning. I don't plan to leave my suite all day tomorrow. I'll have my meals served in and leave Brenda to her own devices. Quite frankly, I need a bit of quiet time to decide what to do about Brenda and Roger's thievery."

"I'll do anything you want me to do," Celia said as she stood up. She wrapped her fingers around the necklace and then impulsively put her arms around Lady Em and kissed her forehead. "Neither one of us deserved what happened to us, but we'll both get past it."

"Yes, we will."

Celia walked to the door and then disappeared into the corridor.

51

The victim of a man who had not only deceived and cheated her, but then tried to tie her to his crime too. Poor Celia, Lady Em thought, as she prepared for bed. I'm glad I gave her the necklace. It will be more secure in the Captain's safe.

Suddenly an overwhelming sense of exhaustion washed over her. I guess I will be able to sleep for a while, she thought, as she began to drift off. About three hours later she was startled awake by the sense that she was not alone in the room. Aided by moonlight and the night light, she was able to see someone moving toward her.

"Who are you? Get out!" she said as something soft came swiftly down and covered her face.

"I can't breathe, I can't breathe—" she tried to say. Desperately, she tried to push away the obstacle that was smothering her, but she was not strong enough.

As she began to lose consciousness, her last thought was that the curse of the Cleopatra necklace had been fulfilled.

Day Four

52

Lady Em had ordered breakfast to be served at eight o'clock. Raymond tapped on the door, then unlocked it and wheeled in the serving cart. The door to the bedroom was half open and he could see that Lady Em was asleep in her bed. Not sure of what to do, he decided to go to his station and phone to tell her that her breakfast had been delivered.

When she did not answer after seven rings, a suspicion began to take root in his mind. Lady Em was old. He had seen the array of medicines in the bathroom closet when he tidied up the suite. Elderly people dying on cruise ships was a regular occurrence.

Before he contacted the doctor, he went back to the suite. He knocked on the partially open door of the bedroom and called her name. When there was no response, he hesitated, then walked into the bedroom. He touched her hand. As he had suspected, it was cold. Lady Emily Haywood was dead. Unnerved, he reached for the phone on the night table.

He could see that her safe was open and jewelry was scattered on the floor. But I'd better leave it there, he thought. I don't need to be accused of stealing. After making the decision, he phoned the ship's doctor.

Sixty-eight years old, with iron-gray hair, Dr. Edwin Blake had retired from his successful practice as a vascular surgeon three years earlier. He was a longtime widower with grown children, and a friend at Castle Line had suggested he might enjoy traveling as the head of the medical facility on an ocean liner. As it turned out, he thoroughly enjoyed that opportunity and was very pleased when he was invited to switch to the *Queen Charlotte*.

After receiving the call from Raymond, he rushed up to Lady Em's suite. At one glance he was able to confirm that she was dead. But then he was immediately concerned by the fact that one arm was dangling off the edge of the bed and the other raised above her head. Bending over closely, he examined her face and observed dried blood at the corner of her mouth.

Suspicious, he looked around and noticed that the other pillow was haphazardly lying on the coverlet. He picked it up and turned it over, then saw a telltale smudge of blood on it. Not wanting to have Raymond even guess his thoughts, he hesitated, then said, "I'm afraid this poor lady suffered a last instant of terrible pain in the heart attack that took her life."

He took Raymond's arm and escorted him out of the bedroom, then shut the door behind them. "I will inform Captain Fairfax of Lady Haywood's passing," he said. "Please be aware that you must not say one word about this to anyone."

The authority in his voice ended Raymond's intention to be on the phone to let all his friends on the staff know what had happened. "Of course, sir," he said, "but it is a very sad occurrence, isn't it? Lady Haywood was a very gracious lady. And to think that only yesterday Mr. Pearson's dreadful accident occurred."

This was no accident, Dr. Blake thought grimly, as he started to leave to speak to the Captain. Then he stopped. "Raymond, I want you to stand guard outside this door. Absolutely no one is to go into this suite until I return. Is that clear?"

"Absolutely. Lady Haywood's assistant has a key. It would be dreadful for her to come in before she is informed of what happened, wouldn't it?"

Or before she tries to destroy any evidence if she's guilty of murder, Edwin Blake thought.

53

Security Chief Saunders, Dr. Blake and Captain Fairfax arrived together at the suite. Before removing the body to the ship's morgue, extensive pictures were taken of Lady Em's face, the position of her right arm and the smear of blood on the pillow.

Their immediate suspicion was that the motive for the murder was robbery. The others watched as Saunders went over to the open safe and looked in it. In addition to the several rings and a bracelet scattered on the floor, he saw that jewelry had been dumped on the shelf. Jewelry pouches were also on the floor, partially hidden by the long evening gowns.

"Is the emerald necklace there?" the Captain asked quietly.

Saunders had seen it on Lady Em's neck at dinner in the dining room. "No sir, it is not. I am even more certain that we are dealing with a robbery, which led to a murder."

54

Gregory Morrison was a flamboyant billionaire whose dream it had been to have a cruise line of his own.

He had been wise enough to not follow his tugboat captain father's advice to skip college and go right to work pulling ocean liners out to sea when he got out of high school. Instead he graduated from college on the dean's list and went on for his MBA. He then worked in Silicon Valley as an analyst, shrewdly discerning which start-up companies offered the most promising new technologies. Fifteen years after forming his own investment fund, he sold it and ended up a billionaire.

Morrison had immediately returned to his goal in life, to own passenger ships. The first one he bought at an auction, then had it refurbished and scheduled its first cruise. Working with a high-powered public relations agency, he courted A-list celebrities from different professions to be part of the inaugural voyage. In exchange for the complimentary cruise, he secured promises from them that they would share their impressions of the trip with their legions of fans on Facebook and Twitter. It had worked. His new cruise line began generating buzz.

Before a year had passed, the vessel was booked two years in advance. The acquisition of second, third and fourth ships soon followed, until the Gregory Morrison River Cruises became the first choice among passengers who loved that kind of travel.

By then Morrison was sixty-three years old. He had acquired a reputation for demanding perfection and would relentlessly steamroll over anyone or anything that stood in his path. Everything he had accomplished until that point was a buildup to his ultimate dream: to create and operate an ocean liner unlike any other, and that would never be surpassed in luxury and elegance.

He particularly wanted to outperform the *Queen Mary*, the *Queen Elizabeth* and the *Rotterdam*. He did not want to have partners or shareholders. The ship he would build would be his masterpiece alone. And when he studied all the appointments of those other ships, he realized that there was one vessel that was the most luxurious ever built, the *Titanic*. He instructed his architect to plan an exact replica of the magnificent staircase and first-class dining room. Included would be old-time amenities, including a gentlemen's smoking room and squash and racquetball courts, as well as an Olympic-sized swimming pool.

Both the suites and the cabins would also be much larger than the ones on rival lines. And the details of the dining rooms would exceed even those on the *Titanic*. The first-class passengers would have sterling silver tableware, and the others silver plate. Only fine china would be used.

As with the *Queen Elizabeth* and the *Queen Mary*, on the walls would be pictures of the British monarchs and members of royalty in European countries. No detail was too small or expensive for Gregory Morrison. And his naming the ship the *Queen Charlotte* was a choice he had made to honor Princess Charlotte, the great-granddaughter of Queen Elizabeth II.

What Gregory had not realized was exactly how much an undertaking like this would burn through even his financial resources. It was absolutely essential that the maiden voyage be a glorious success.

He could have bitten his tongue a thousand times after allowing the PR firm to mention the name *Titanic* in its press releases. The press ignored the fact that the reference was to the splendor of the *Titanic*, not her ill-fated maiden voyage.

During the first three days of the voyage Gregory Morrison constantly was vigilant for even the smallest detail that might be short of perfection.

A bulky six-footer with piercing brown eyes and a full head of silver hair, Morrison was a formidable figure. Everyone was afraid of him, from the chef and his assistants to the clerks behind the various desks, to the attendants in the restaurants and suites. That was why when Captain Fairfax asked to see him, Morrison's first question was "Is anything wrong?"

"I think we should have the discussion in the privacy of your suite, sir."

"I hope you're not going to tell me another passenger has gone overboard," Morrison thundered. "Come up immediately."

He already had the door open when Captain Fairfax, John Saunders and Dr. Blake arrived together. When he saw Dr. Blake, he asked, "Don't tell me somebody else is dead!" he exclaimed.

"I'm afraid it's worse than that, Mr. Morrison," the Captain said. "It's not just somebody. It's Lady Emily Haywood who was found dead in the bedroom of her suite this morning."

"Lady Emily Haywood!" Morrison exploded. "What happened to her?"

It was Dr. Blake who answered. "Lady Haywood did not die of natural causes. She was suffocated by a pillow that was held over her face. There is absolutely no doubt in my mind that it was a homicide."

Morrison's face was normally ruddy, as though he had been in a cold wind. Now as the other three men watched, it paled to a pasty gray.

Clenching and unclenching his fists, he asked, "She was wearing the Cleopatra necklace last night. Did you find it in her room?"

"The safe was open and her jewelry was dumped out of it. The Cleopatra necklace was missing," Saunders said quietly.

For a long minute Morrison said nothing. His first thoughts were of how to keep the news of her murder quiet. And of the terrible publicity that would inevitably follow if word leaked out.

"Who else knows about this?" he asked.

"Besides the four of us, Raymond Broad, the butler to Lady Em's suite. He was the one who found the body. I told him that I believed she had died of natural causes," Dr. Blake said.

"The fact that she was murdered absolutely must *not* leave this room. Captain Fairfax, you will compose a message to be broadcast saying that she passed away peacefully in her sleep. And not one word about the missing necklace."

"If I can make a suggestion, Mr. Morrison, when the authorities come on board in Southampton, their first question will be what we did to preserve the crime scene and to control who entered or left her suite so that any potential evidence would be preserved. That said, we will have to go back to the suite to remove the body to the morgue," Saunders said.

"Can we wait until the middle of the night to remove the body?" Morrison asked.

"Sir, that would not be wise and might arouse suspicion," Dr. Blake said. "Since we must announce the death, it would not seem unusual that the body, covered of course, would be moved to the ship's morgue."

"Take her down when most passengers are at lunch," Morrison ordered. "What do we know about the butler, Raymond Broad?" he asked.

Saunders responded. "As I said before, he is the one who discovered her body. The previous evening she had requested breakfast in her room and he was delivering it. By the time he found her, she had been dead for at least five to six hours. Whoever committed the crime did so at approximately three o'clock in the morning. About Mr. Broad, he has worked at your companies for fifteen years, including his time at Morrison River Cruises. He has never been linked to any infractions."

"Whoever did this, did they break into her room?"

"There's no sign of any damage to her door lock."

"Who else would have had a key to her room?"

"We know her longtime assistant Brenda Martin had a duplicate key," Saunders said. "But if I may remind you, the international thief, the so-called Man with One Thousand Faces, is rumored to be aboard the ship. In fact, if the Internet is to be believed, he has even announced his presence here. Someone of his ingenuity would know a way to bypass her door lock and gain entrance to her safe."

"Why was I not told that a jewel thief was on board?" Morrison roared.

This time it was Fairfax who responded. "I did send a note to you, sir, informing you that a member of Interpol traveling as a guest is here to provide additional security."

"Well, obviously the idiot is doing a great job!"

"Sir," Saunders inquired, "should we notify the legal department and ask for their guidance?"

"I don't want their guidance," Morrison exploded. "I want to get to Southampton on time with no more incidents and get that damn body off my ship."

"Another thing, sir. Presumably, the jewelry on the floor is very valuable. If we leave it there, we run the risk of it," he paused, "disappearing. If we go in and retrieve it—"

"I know," Morrison interrupted. "We run the risk of unnecessarily disturbing a crime scene."

"I did take the liberty, sir, of posting a guard outside the door to her suite," Saunders said.

Morrison ignored him. "You're sure there's no chance this butler did it? If he did it, I don't want to know about it. You know, or should know, that if an employee is guilty of the crime, I as owner of the ship am absolutely liable in any lawsuits that may be filed." Morrison began to pace up and down the room squeezing his hands into fists. "We know about this Brenda Martin, her assistant," he said. "Besides her, who else was traveling in Lady Haywood's party?"

"Roger Pearson, the man who fell overboard, was her financial advisor and the executor of her estate; he and his wife Yvonne and Brenda Martin were the guests of Lady Haywood."

"I saw the people at her dinner table," Morrison said. "Who was that beautiful young woman? I met her at the cocktail party, but I can't remember her name."

"It's Celia Kilbride. She is one of our guest lecturers, as is Professor Longworth," Saunders said.

"Her topic is the history of famous gems," Captain Fairfax added.

"Mr. Morrison," Saunders said, "I believe it would be wise for me to speak to the passengers who were in the suites near Lady Haywood's to see if they heard any sounds of a disturbance or saw anyone in the hallway outside her suite."

"Not on your life. That will be a dead giveaway that something is wrong. We're not trying to solve a crime. I don't care who did it, as long as it's not an employee." Morrison paused, deep in thought. "Go over with me again what the butler said."

Saunders replied, "His name is Raymond Broad. He tells a pretty straight story. As you know, when a meal is ordered for a certain time, our butlers, after tapping on the door, are permitted to enter the suite and leave the meal cart. This is a particularly necessary service for our older guests, many of whom are hard of hearing. Since the door to Lady Em's bedroom was open, he says he glanced in, saw that she was still in bed, and then called out to her that her breakfast had been served. When she didn't respond, he went back to his station, phoned her room, but got no answer. He thought that something must be wrong, returned to her suite and stepped inside the bedroom. Then he could see that the door to her safe was open and jewelry scattered on the floor. He went over to the bed and realized she did not appear to be breathing. He touched her hand and said her skin felt cold. That was when he used the suite phone to call Dr. Blake."

"Tell him if he wants to keep his job he better keep his mouth shut about what he saw in that suite. Make it damn clear to him that she died in her sleep. That's all."

55

Professor Longworth was sitting alone at the breakfast table when he was joined by Brenda Martin. *A woman I find particularly dull,* he thought, as he stood up courteously and greeted her with a smile.

"And how is Lady Em this morning?" he asked. "I was concerned for her last evening. She looked very pale."

"When I didn't hear from her by nine o'clock, it meant that she was having breakfast in her suite," Brenda replied. The waiter was at her side. She ordered her usual generous breakfast of orange juice, cantaloupe, poached eggs hollandaise, sausage and coffee.

It was then that Yvonne Pearson arrived at the table. "I couldn't bear to be alone any longer," she explained, her voice breaking. "I wanted to be with friends." She had worn almost no makeup to accentuate her supposedly grief-stricken appearance. Not having carried any black clothes in her wardrobe, she'd done the next best thing. She was wearing a gray running suit. Her only jewelry was her diamond wedding band. She had slept soundly and knew that she did not portray the exhausted look that would have been most suitable. But as the waiter held her chair for her, she sighed. "I cried all night. All I could think of was my darling Roger falling. If only he had listened to me. I begged him often not to sit on the railing." She brushed away an imaginary tear as she sat down and picked up the menu.

Brenda nodded sympathetically, but Professor Longworth, a keen student of human nature, saw through the façade. She's a good actress, he thought. I don't think those two were happy with each other. It was clear there was tension between them. Roger was always fawning over Lady Em, and Yvonne didn't hide the fact that she was bored with both of them.

At that moment the Captain's somber announcement that Lady Em had passed away in her sleep was heard throughout the ship.

Brenda gasped, "Oh no," stood up and ran from the dining room. "Why didn't they tell me? Why didn't they tell me?"

Henry Longworth and Yvonne Pearson exchanged shocked glances and then stared numbly at their plates.

At their table Alvirah, Willy, Anna DeMille and Devon Michaelson reacted to the announcement with disbelief. It was Anna who spoke first. "Two people dead in two days," she gasped, "and my mother had a saying, 'Death comes in threes.' "

Alvirah was the one who responded. "I've heard that too, but I'm sure it's just an old wives' tale."

At least I pray it is, she thought to herself.

56

It had been virtually impossible for Celia to fall asleep. The responsibility of holding the Cleopatra necklace for even a few overnight hours was overwhelming. The fact that Lady Em's assistant, Brenda Martin, and her financial advisor, Roger Pearson, had probably been stealing from her was sickening. How miserable it must be to be eighty-six years old and realize that people you felt to be both close friends and well-paid employees could treat you like that. It's such a shame that Lady Em doesn't have any close relatives, Celia thought.

And neither do I was her next dismal thought. Since the terrible situation had begun, she had started to miss her father more and more. In a crazy way she was resentful that he had never remarried and that she might have had siblings. Half-siblings, she corrected herself, but that would be good enough for me. She knew that only a few of the friends who had invested in Steven's hedge fund believed that she had been part of his scheme. Nevertheless, almost all of them had been visibly cool to her. The money they had been saving for the new house or condo or to start a family had vanished. Guilt by association, she thought bitterly, as her eyes finally began to close.

The sleep that finally did come had resulted in five hours of deep, heavy slumber. It was nine-thirty when she was finally awakened by the voice of Captain Fairfax. "It is with great regret that we announce the passing of Lady Emily Haywood some time during the night. . . ."

Lady Em is *dead*! That's impossible, Celia thought. She sat up and got out of bed, her thoughts racing. Do they know that the Cleopatra necklace is missing? Would they have immediately opened her safe to look for it? What will they think if I just go right to the Captain now, give him the necklace, and explain the circumstances under which Lady Em gave it to me?

As she was thinking the problem through, she began to calm down. By giving the necklace to the Captain, she would show that she is not a thief. What thief would go to the trouble of stealing something and then hours later give it back?

Stop being so paranoid, she told herself. Everything will be fine.

Her thoughts were interrupted by the sound of the phone ringing. It was her lawyer, Randolph Knowles. "Celia, I'm sorry to tell you this. I just spoke to the FBI. They definitely want to interview you as soon as you get back to New York."

She had barely hung up when the phone rang again. It was Alvirah. "Celia, I didn't want you to be blindsided. I've been watching the morning news. The story in *People* is being reported already." She paused. "And you must have heard the Captain's announcement that Lady Em had passed away."

"Yes, I did."

"Of course the Captain didn't admit it, but it's all over the news that she was murdered and the priceless Cleopatra necklace is missing."

When the call ended, Celia drifted to the couch and sat down in stunned silence. Lady Em murdered? she thought. And the necklace missing? She tried to remain calm even as the stunning implications of what that meant for her exploded in her consciousness.

I have the necklace, she thought frantically. I was in Lady Em's room hours before she died, before she was murdered. Will anyone believe Lady Em gave it to me? With that story in *People* coming out today with Steven swearing I was in on the hedge fund fraud with him, who would believe that I wouldn't steal if given the opportunity? Any crooked antiquities dealer would pay a fortune for the necklace, then sell it to one of those private collectors who want a treasure like that for their own satisfaction. Or those incredible emeralds could be sold one by one to jewelers. And who would have the connections to arrange a private sale? As a gemologist who travels the world, I would.

She went to her safe, removed the necklace and gazed at the flawless emeralds. It was hard for her to fathom that she was actively considering whether she should go out on the balcony and toss it into the ocean below.

57

When Brenda reached Lady Em's suite, she found a guard at the door. "I'm sorry, ma'am, by order of the Captain no one will be permitted to enter this room until we dock in Southampton."

Frustrated, Brenda said, "I have been Lady Em's personal assistant for twenty years. Surely I can—"

The guard cut her off. "I'm sorry, ma'am, Captain's orders."

Brenda turned abruptly and walked down the corridor, her rigid back expressing her outrage to the guard. That's the way I would act if I gave a damn about her, she thought. Now no more shuffling behind her, anticipating her every whim or need.

Ralphie! Now she could be with him all the time. Now she wouldn't have to hide him because she knew Lady Em would not approve of him. The apartment she and Ralphie live in belonged to Lady Em. It wouldn't have killed her to leave it to me. Who knows how long whoever manages her estate will let me stay there? In the meantime, it's rent-free. I'll just stay until somebody tells me to get out.

Her thoughts went back to Lady Em. She is leaving me three hundred thousand dollars, Brenda thought. And we have two million from switching and selling the jewelry. Free! I'm free of all the kowtowing I've been doing all these years.

At least during the valuation of all her jewelry I don't have to worry about someone asking why so many pieces are cheap. Maybe they'll think that with everything she bought over the years, she might have been taken by a crooked jeweler who sold her the junk. Lady Em insured only the jewelry that was worth more than one hundred thousand dollars. Those are the pieces they'll focus on. Ralphie and I luckily stayed away from the insured jewelry.

Brenda reassured herself with that thought until it occurred to her that Lady Em might have asked Celia Kilbride to take a look at her "picnic" bracelet. I should find out a little more about this gemologist, Brenda thought to herself, as she opened her laptop. She typed *Celia Kilbride* into Google. The first story that appeared was about Celia's potential link to her former fiancé's hedge fund swindle. But Brenda's eyes widened as she saw another headline exclaiming "Philanthropist Lady Emily Haywood Murdered on Luxury Cruise Ship."

After quickly scanning the story, she closed her computer. She felt herself breathing rapidly. I was going to be okay, she thought, if Lady Em had died in her sleep. That's what old people do. If they're right and she was murdered, will that change the way they look at me?

It might provide cover for me and Ralphie. The article had said that the Cleopatra necklace was missing. That means the killer probably got into Lady Em's safe. Unless he's caught, nobody will know how much jewelry or which pieces were stolen. If I'm asked, I can say that Lady Em used to make copies of various pieces of her jewelry. She brought a number of legitimate pieces and a number of copies on the trip. The thief must have taken some of the good stuff and left the junk.

Brenda was now feeling infinitely better. That also explains the guard at the door of her suite and not letting me in, she thought. The ship was trying to cover up the murder and theft by saying she died of natural causes.

Lady Em's gone and I have an alibi regarding the jewelry, but I'm not completely home free.

If Lady Em told Celia she suspected I had substituted the bracelet, would Celia tell that to the police when the ship docked? Or would she tell the Captain now, and will the police be waiting for me? If Lady Em was murdered, would Celia feel even more compelled to report anything Lady Em told her? But will Celia have any credibility because of the fund swindle?

If she tells them anything, it will be her word against mine, Brenda told herself nervously, as she returned to the dining room and asked the waiter to bring her a fresh cup of coffee and a blueberry muffin. Five minutes later, after she had taken a big bite of her muffin, her jaw froze. I'm the only one who has a key to Lady Em's suite. Is anybody going to think I might have killed her?

58

Ted Cavanaugh was finishing breakfast and winding up a telephone conversation with his law partner when the announcement of Lady Haywood's death came over the public address system. He was holding a cup of coffee and had to grasp it tightly to keep from dropping it.

He felt sorry for Lady Em, but his next thought was, I hope that the Cleopatra necklace is safe. I wonder if word of her death has reached the press, he thought, as he began tapping on his iPhone. It certainly had.

"Lady Emily Haywood Murdered and Famous Necklace May Be Missing" was the headline on Yahoo News. That can't be true, he thought, even as he realized there must have been some verification. The Captain's announcement had said nothing about murder. There are always wild rumors online, but he guessed this was too extraordinary to not be true. The story went on to say that in the early hours of this morning, Lady Haywood had been smothered with a pillow as she lay in bed. It said that her safe was open and jewelry was scattered on the floor.

The Cleopatra necklace. What a tragedy if it was lost. It was the last piece of jewelry Cleopatra had sent for as she prepared to commit suicide rather than be taken prisoner by Octavian.

He thought of the antiquities he and his law partners had recovered for the rightful owners. Paintings for the families of Auschwitz victims. Paintings and sculptures for the Louvre museum that had been stolen when France was occupied in World War II. And they had successfully sued antiques and art dealers who had peddled to unsuspecting buyers copies of valuable artifacts as if they were the real thing.

His mind raced as he thought of the people on the ship who were close to Lady Em.

Brenda Martin, of course.

Roger Pearson, but he was dead. Were Lady Em and Pearson's widow close?

How about Celia Kilbride? Lady Em had attended her lectures, chatted with her when they ended and invited the gemologist to sit at her table.

He typed "Celia Kilbride" into Google. The lead story was a *People* magazine interview with her accused former fiancé, who swore she was in on his swindle.

As a lawyer he knew that after the release of the interview the FBI would be compelled to take a closer look at her potential involvement in the theft. Her legal fees must be exorbitant.

Could she have been driven to steal the necklace? If she stole it, how did she get into Lady Em's room?

He tried to imagine what had transpired in Lady Em's suite. Did Lady Em wake up and find her opening the safe?

And if that happened, would Celia Kilbride have panicked, grabbed a pillow and smothered Lady Em?

But even as all this occurred to him, Ted could visualize Celia Kilbride coming into the cocktail party last night, looking absolutely beautiful as she warmly greeted other people in the room.

59

With increasing despair, Roger Pearson had watched the sun come up. His arms were leaden. His teeth were chattering. A cold rain had provided essential freshwater for him to gulp, but left his whole body shivering.

It was an effort to keep his arms and legs moving. He knew that if he was not in hypothermia, he was very close to it. He didn't know if he would have the energy to re-inflate the pants he was using as a flotation device when the remaining air escaped. I can't last much longer, he thought.

And then he thought he saw it. Some type of ship coming his way. He had long ago given up any semblance of religion, but now he found himself praying. Dear God, let somebody be looking this way. Let someone see me.

There are no atheists in foxholes was his last conscious thought, while forcing himself not to wave until he was in visual range of the ship. Now he was struggling to keep afloat in the swells that had suddenly begun to choke his nostrils and push him away from the oncoming vessel.

60

Alvirah and Willy were deep in conversation as they put in their daily mile and a half stroll on the promenade deck. "Willy, there was always the risk of someone stealing the Cleopatra necklace, but for someone to smother that poor lady to get it is so awful."

"Greed is an awful motive," Willy said somberly, then noticed that Alvirah was wearing the sapphire ring he had given her for their forty-fifth wedding anniversary. "Honey, you never wear any jewelry during the day except your wedding ring," he commented. "How come you're sporting the new one?"

"Because I don't intend to have anyone sneak into our stateroom and steal it," Alvirah replied. "And I'll bet most of the people on this ship are doing the same thing. And if they don't want to wear it, they'll be carrying it in their handbags. Oh Willy, to think how this cruise was perfection for the first few days. And then poor Roger Pearson fell overboard and now Lady Em was murdered. Who would have believed it?"

Willy did not answer. He was looking at the dark clouds that were forming overhead and feeling the increased side-to-side rolling motion of the ship. I wouldn't be surprised if we're going into heavy weather, he thought. If we do, I hope it won't start to feel like the *Titanic*: luxury upon luxury, only to end in disaster.

What a crazy thought. He chided himself as he reached for Alvirah's hand and gave it a squeeze.

61

The Man with One Thousand Faces had listened grimly as the Captain announced Lady Em's death over the ship's public address system.

I'm sorry I had to kill her, he thought. It was for nothing. The necklace was gone. It wasn't in the safe. I searched through all the drawers in the bedroom. I didn't have time to look in the living room. But I'm certain she would not have left it there.

Where is it? Who has it? Anyone on this ship could have followed her and seen her enter her suite. Who else would have had a key to her suite?

As he paced around the promenade deck, he began to calm down and plan. The kind of people on this trip certainly aren't the type who would steal a necklace, he decided.

She obviously didn't feel well at dinner. Anyone who was watching her as closely as I was could see that. Would her assistant, Brenda, have gone up to the suite after dinner? It was possible, even probable.

It appeared that there was some strain between her and Lady Em. Was Brenda the one who had the necklace now?

Ahead of him on the deck he caught sight of the Meehans. Instinct told him to be careful of Alvirah. He had looked her up. She better not try to solve *this* crime, he thought.

He slowed his pace so as not to catch up with them. He needed time to think, to plan. There were only three days left until they would reach Southampton, and there was no way he was leaving this ship without the Cleopatra necklace.

And Brenda was the only one whom he was sure had a key to Lady Em's suite. He knew what his next move would have to be.

62

Celia ran for an hour, then showered, dressed and sent for coffee and a muffin. The words "what shall I do?" were swirling through her mind. Suppose I go to the Captain and give him the necklace, she asked herself, will he believe me? And if he doesn't, will he lock me in the brig? Can I wipe my fingerprints off it and leave it someplace where it would be found? That's one possibility. But suppose someone sees me or it is caught on camera? What then? Would they be allowed to search the cabins for it? No, if they had done that, they would have already found the necklace in my safe.

Panicked at that thought, Celia looked around the room frantically. She went to the safe, opened it and took out the Cleopatra necklace. She had dressed for her lecture and was wearing a jacket and slacks. The jacket was the flowing style with one wide button at the neck. The slacks had deep pockets. Could she possibly keep the necklace on her person? Her hands trembled as she shoved the bulky piece into the left-hand pocket and ran to the mirror.

There was no bulge showing.

It's the best I can do, she thought despairingly.

63

Kim Volpone liked nothing better than taking a walk before breakfast. She was sailing on *Paradise*, a ship that was headed for her first stop, Southampton. A hard overnight rain had subsided and the sun had just popped through. The deck was almost void of passengers.

As she walked, she inhaled deeply. She loved the smell of the fresh ocean breeze. Forty years old and freshly divorced, she was cruising with her closest friend, Laura Bruno, and experiencing a sense of great relief that the nasty business of dividing assets was over. Her husband Walter had turned out to be a Walter Mitty type, pipe dreams instead of reality.

Midway through the walk, she stopped and looked out over the horizon. She squinted her eyes and blinked. What was that she was seeing? Was it some of the floating garbage that unfortunately found its way into these waters? Maybe, but something appeared to be moving back and forth.

About twenty feet from her was an older man standing with his arm around a woman near his age. Around his neck was a strap holding a pair of binoculars.

"Excuse me, sir, I don't believe we've met. I'm Kim Volpone."

"I'm Ralph Mittl, and this is my wife Mildred."

"Would it be possible, Ralph, to borrow your binoculars?"

Reluctantly, he agreed. "Please be careful," he admonished her. "They're very expensive."

"I will be," Kim promised absently, as she took them from his hands. She put the strap around her neck and adjusted the lenses. When she focused on the moving object, she caught her breath. It appeared to be an arm flailing back and forth. She gasped, pulled the strap from around her neck, and handed the binoculars back to their owner.

"Look over there," she said as she pointed. "What do you see?"

Surprised at the urgency in her voice, he took the binoculars, readjusted them to his vision and directed them toward the horizon. "There's someone out there," he exclaimed and turned back to her.

"I'll keep watching," he said. "Go tell a crew member to call the Captain. There's someone in the water. He's trying to signal our ship."

Ten minutes later, a boat with four crewmen aboard had been lowered and was speeding toward whoever was in the water.

64

Captain Fairfax and John Saunders had answered Morrison's shouted commands to come to his suite at once. "How did that story leak out?" an apoplectic Morrison demanded. "Who told them what happened?"

"I can only assume that the Man with One Thousand Faces was the source," Saunders answered.

"How about Dr. Blake? How about the butler?"

Captain Fairfax stiffened but tried not to let his anger show.

"If my life depended on it, I would say that Dr. Blake would never reveal that information. As for Raymond Broad, as I told you, I am not even sure he was aware of the fact that Lady Haywood was the victim of foul play. If I were to make a guess, I would agree with what Mr. Saunders just said. This is likely another example of the Man with One Thousand Faces bragging to the media."

"Wait a minute. What about that guy, the detective from Interpol? What's his name?" Morrison said, the creases in his forehead deepening.

"It's Devon Michaelson, sir," Captain Fairfax replied.

"Tell him I want him to get up here now. And I mean right now," Morrison thundered.

Without answering, Fairfax reached for the phone. "Ring me Devon Michaelson's suite," he said. Three rings later he picked up. "Mr. Michaelson, this is Captain Fairfax. I'm in Mr. Morrison's suite. He wants you to come up immediately and meet with him."

"Of course. I know where it is. I'll be right there."

For a long three minutes there was an uncomfortable silence. It was broken when Devon Michaelson tapped on the door and opened it.

Morrison wasted no time on pleasantries. "I hear you're with Interpol," he said abruptly. "We've had a murder and a piece of priceless jewelry stolen. Weren't you supposed to prevent that?"

Michaelson did not attempt to hide the anger in his face. "Mr. Morrison," he said, his tone icy, "I assume you will provide me with the security tapes from the dining area and the hallways leading to where Lady Haywood's suite is located."

Captain Fairfax answered, "Mr. Michaelson, you are probably not aware of the situation on most cruise liners. Because we value the privacy of our guests, we do not place cameras in the hallways."

"Well, that means you are also protecting the privacy of a thief and a murderer. Did it occur to you that with the valuables your guests have in their very expensive suites, it might have been appropriate to have a security guard present at all times?"

"Don't you tell me how to run my ship," Morrison snapped. "Guards everywhere! I'm running a luxury liner, not a prison. Now, I'm sure that you are a very fine detective and by now you have solved this case. Why don't you tell us all what happened?"

Michaelson's tone was equally icy. "I can tell you that I am taking a very close look at several people."

"I want to know who they are," Morrison demanded.

"Experience has taught me to first focus on the individual who found the body. Very often that person is not saying as much as he knows. I am probing further into the background of your butler, Raymond Broad."

"I assure you that every employee on this ship was thoroughly investigated before being hired," Saunders insisted.

"I'm sure they were," Michaelson said. "But *I assure you* that Interpol's investigative resources vastly surpass those available to you."

"Who else?" Morrison asked.

"There are several other passengers whose backgrounds are of interest to me. For now I will share the name of only one. Mr. Edward Cavanaugh."

"The ambassador's son?" Fairfax asked with dismay.

"Ted, as he calls himself, Cavanaugh, travels extensively in Europe and the Middle East. I have reviewed his flight records, passport stamps and hotel records. By coincidence or otherwise, he has been in close proximity to the scenes of the Man with One Thousand Faces thefts over the past seven years. And he has openly indicated his interest in the so-called Cleopatra necklace.

"And now having answered your questions, I will take my leave."

As the door closed behind Michaelson, Captain Fairfax said, "Mr. Morrison, another matter. I have been inundated with calls and emails from the press seeking comment on how Lady Em died and if the Cleopatra necklace has been stolen. How do you want me to reply?"

"We stick to our story that Lady Em died of natural causes, period," Morrison shot back.

Fairfax asked, "We do know that the Cleopatra necklace is missing. Should we not warn the passengers to be careful with their valuables?"

"Not one word about missing or stolen jewelry," Morrison snapped. "That's all."

The two men took that as a dismissal and left the suite.

Even though it was only ten o'clock in the morning, Gregory Morrison went to the suite bar and poured himself a generous glass of vodka. He was not given to praying, but he was thinking, Dear God, don't let it be an employee who killed her.

Ten minutes later Morrison received a call from his firm's public relations office. He was told that in addition to the rumor that Lady Em was murdered and her necklace was stolen, there were news reports saying that because of the story in *People*, Celia Kilbride was going to be questioned by the FBI again over her involvement in a hedge fund fraud. Since she was a guest lecturer on *Queen Charlotte*, he and the Captain should be ready to respond to questions from passengers.

"I certainly ought to know," Morrison barked. He hung up the phone and called for his chief of security to come back to his suite.

When Saunders arrived, in a deadly calm voice, Morrison asked, "Were you aware that one of our lecturers, Celia Kilbride, is under suspicion for being involved in a fraud?"

"No, I was not. The lecturers are booked by the entertainment director. Most of my focus, naturally, is on the passengers and Castle Line employees."

"When is Kilbride due to lecture again?"

Saunders took out his iPhone, tapped it several times, and replied, "This afternoon in the theater. But it's not another lecture; it's a conversation with Mr. Breidenbach, the entertainment director, and she'll also answer questions from the audience."

"Well, tell her to forget it. That's all I need is for people to know that I hired a thief to give a talk on my ship!"

Saunders replied carefully, "Mr. Morrison, I believe it is in our best interests to keep things as normal as possible for the balance of the voyage. Do you realize that if we cancel Ms. Kilbride's appearance, in addition to disappointing the passengers who are planning to attend, we would be announcing that we suspect her of the theft and murder in Lady Haywood's suite? Is this what we want to do?"

"She's a gemologist, isn't she?"

"Yes, she is."

"So that means the talk will be about jewelry, right? Has it occurred to you that most of the passengers at the talk will know that Kilbride is being investigated for participating in a swindle?"

"I would say, yes, they'll know. However, in essence, since *we* know there was a homicide on board, and the Interpol agent did not mention her, you would also by default be saying that you think she was involved. There could be very unpleasant repercussions. If it turns out she is not guilty, she might come after you for defamation of character. I strongly, strongly suggest that you do not cancel her scheduled presentation."

Morrison considered. "Okay, if she's up onstage for an hour, at least I'll know she's not in some other old lady's suite killing her and stealing more jewelry. Leave it as scheduled. I will make it my business to be there to hear her."

65

At twenty past three Celia stood in the wings of the auditorium. Peering around the curtain, she could see that almost every seat had been taken. Alvirah and Willy Meehan, Ted Cavanaugh, Devon Michaelson and Anna DeMille were in the front row. Also in the front row was a man she recognized as Gregory Morrison, the owner of the *Queen Charlotte*. Why is he here? she wondered, her mouth suddenly dry.

The thought crossed her mind that a day ago Lady Emily had been in the first row as well. Involuntarily, her hand clutched the pocket where the bulky necklace was hidden.

She heard her name being announced by Anthony Breidenbach, the entertainment director. Attempting a smile, she walked onstage and shook his hand as he spoke. "Celia Kilbride is a renowned gemologist from Carruthers in New York. Her expertise in appraising valuable gems as well as her knowledge of the history of their background has fascinated us in her previous lectures. Today is a little bit different. She will be answering questions from me, and afterward, the audience." Celia and the entertainment director walked to chairs that were facing each other and sat down.

"Celia, my first question is about birthstones and what they symbolize. Let's start with amber."

"Amber is a stone astrologically linked with the zodiac sign of Taurus. Early physicians prescribed wearing it to ward off headaches, heart problems and many other ailments. Ancient Egyptians placed a piece of amber with their dead to assure that the body would remain whole," Celia answered, comfortable now that she was on familiar ground.

"How about aquamarine?"

"That is the March birthstone, Pisces. It is thought to bring joy and happiness, and harmony in married life. The ancient Greeks thought it was sacred to their god Poseidon. It's a great stone to take on vacations and cruises."

"Let's go to some of the really expensive stones," the entertainment director said. "How about diamonds?"

"The diamond is the April birthstone, Aries." Celia smiled. "It's believed to bring forth purity, harmony, love and abundance. Those lucky enough to afford to buy one believed it made them safe from the plague."

"What about the emerald?"

"Emerald is also a stone of Taurus. It is the May birthstone. It is supposed to secure love and attract wealth. During the Renaissance emeralds were exchanged among the aristocracy as symbols of friendship. It is the sacred stone of the goddess Venus."

"One more. Tell us about gold."

"It doesn't have its own spot on the astrology calendar. It is intimately linked with divinity and those gods associated with the sun. It is a symbol of good health. Gold earrings were thought to strengthen the eyes, and among sailors and fishermen to prevent one from drowning."

The moment she finished that sentence, Celia thought of Roger Pearson. If the entertainment director had the same thought, he did not show it.

"All right, now it's the audience's turn," Breidenbach said. "Please raise your hand if you have a question. My assistant will bring the microphone to you."

Celia had been concerned that the first question would be about the Cleopatra necklace. Instead it was from a woman who asked about the emerald-and-diamond necklace Sir Alexander Korda had purchased for the actress Merle Oberon in 1939.

"That necklace was magnificent," Celia told her. "It had twenty-nine emeralds. It is believed they are the same shape and size, the same stones in fact, as those that previously adorned regal maharajas in India in the fifteenth century."

As soon as Celia finished, at least a dozen hands went up. The questions followed in quick succession: "What is the history of the Hope diamond?" "What about the jewels in the British coronation crown?" "Was it true that the tradition of giving diamond engagement rings resulted from a successful De Beers marketing campaign in the 1930s?" One that brought a laugh was "Was the ring that was stolen from Kim Kardashian worth four million dollars?"

It was at the very end of the session that a question was asked about the Cleopatra necklace. "Was it really stolen and was Lady Haywood murdered?"

"I have no idea if the necklace was stolen," Celia answered. "And I have no reason to believe the rumor that Lady Haywood's death was not from natural causes."

Score one for you, Morrison thought. He felt relieved that he had decided to allow Kilbride's presentation to go forward. That is, until the final questions.

"Ms. Kilbride, many of us, including you, were at the Captain's cocktail party and the dinner that followed. We saw Lady Emily wearing the Cleopatra necklace. Despite the widely circulated rumors that it has been stolen, the ship insists it was not. Can you confirm this?"

"No one from the ship has contacted me about the necklace," Celia said uncomfortably.

"And wasn't there a curse on the necklace that said anyone who brought it to sea would not reach shore alive?"

Celia's mind was filled with the thought of Lady Em joking about the curse. "Yes," she said. "According to legend, a curse along those lines is associated with the necklace."

"Thank you, Celia Kilbride, and thank you to everyone in our audience," Breidenbach said as he stood up and the audience began to applaud.

66

Yvonne, Valerie Conrad and Dana Terrace had attended Celia's lecture. Afterward they went down to the Edwardian Bar for a cocktail. Yvonne had explained to her friends that she simply could not bear to be alone in her suite. "Every moment that I'm in there," she said, her voice trembling and sad, "I see Roger. And I live again that terrible moment when he leaned back, then raised his arms as he fell. I was at the door of the balcony and I warned him, 'Roger, please don't sit on the railing. You'll fall overboard.'

"He laughed and said, 'Don't worry, I'm a good swimmer.' " She managed to squeeze a tear out of her right eye.

Valerie and Dana cooed in sympathy. "It must have been so awful for you," Valerie said. "I can't imagine anything so horrible," Dana joined in.

"I'll have to live with that memory every day of my life," Yvonne lamented.

"Have you thought about funeral arrangements or a memorial service?" Dana asked.

"I've barely been able to think straight," Yvonne said. "But of course I'll have a memorial service. I think two weeks from now would be appropriate under the circumstances." And by then I should have the insurance money, Yvonne thought.

"I heard about the ceremony where the man scattered his wife's ashes," Dana said.

"At least he had her ashes to throw over," Yvonne replied.

"Yvonne, we hope you're going to be okay," Valerie said as she patted Yvonne's hand. "Did Roger have life insurance?"

"Yes, he did, thank God. He had a five-million-dollar policy. But, of course, we have other assets, stocks and bonds."

"Well, that's good because I'm pretty sure the insurance company won't pay right away unless the body is recovered."

Yvonne hadn't thought of that potential delay. She made a silent prayer of thanksgiving that Lady Em had been murdered before she was able to order an outside review of her finances.

"Yvonne, it's much too early to say this, but try to look ahead," Valerie said. "You're attractive. You're young. You don't have children or other baggage. You'll be a wealthy widow. I'm sorry about poor Roger, but there is a bright side to all this. If you had been divorced, you would have had to split everything with Roger. This way you get it all."

"Oh, I never thought of it like that," Yvonne murmured, as she shook her head.

"We'll be on the lookout for a suitable guy for you," Dana promised.

Having settled Yvonne's future over a second cocktail, they turned their attention to Celia Kilbride.

"That lecture was actually very interesting," Yvonne said.

"She certainly doesn't look like anyone who would suffocate an old woman," Valerie observed. "You were sitting with her, Yvonne. What was your impression of her when you met her with the other people at the table?"

"Pretty quiet, but I guess she has a lot on her mind. I wouldn't want to be interrogated by the FBI." And I would be if Lady Em were still alive, she thought. For all I know Roger might have included my name on some of the documents he used to cover the theft. If Celia *is* the one who killed Lady Em, I say, "God bless her."

"If Celia has the necklace, what is she going to do with it?" Dana asked. "I mean it's priceless. But unless she sells it to a Saudi prince, I don't know who would buy it."

"My guess is that she'd break it up into individual emeralds," Valerie chimed in. "She'd get a fortune for every one of them. Don't forget, she's in the business. She must know plenty of buyers who wouldn't question the source."

The three turned their attention to Ted Cavanaugh. "Beyond handsome," they agreed.

"And did you notice how he was trying to get close to Lady Em? The first night when Lady Em took a seat at a table, he rushed to get the table next to hers," Yvonne said. "I was sitting next to Lady Em and I could see that he almost knocked over people to grab the table to our left. He sat with the lottery winners, Devon Michaelson, the bereaved widower who probably had a girlfriend even before his wife's death, and the church lady from the Midwest . . ." Her voice trailed off.

"What about the Shakespeare guy?" Dana asked.

"The one whose eyebrows keep going up and down," Valerie suggested as she imitated him with her own eyebrows.

"Exactly," Dana verified. "I would say he doesn't look like the type of person who would kill anyone."

"No, but he sure enjoys talking about murder," Yvonne insisted. Her voice deepened, " '*Out, damn spot! Out, I say! Will all the waters in the ocean wash this blood from my hands?*' Or something like that."

Dana and Valerie went into gales of laughter. "You do a great Lady Macbeth," Dana said. "Now, what's wrong with having another Manhattan cocktail?"

"Absolutely nothing," Valerie agreed as she signaled for the waiter.

67

Ted Cavanaugh attended the jewelry discussion and was impressed by Celia's speaking skills as she answered all the questions that were tossed at her. He was also once again aware of the fact that she was a beautiful woman. And he admired her poise as she handled a question about Lady Em's death.

Everyone in the audience had to have been aware of the *People* article and its allegation from her former fiancé that she conspired with him on the theft, Ted thought.

After it was over, a number of people in the audience waited to speak with her. As the last one left, Ted got up and stopped Celia near the door. They had exchanged greetings at the cocktail party, but that was all.

He said, "Celia, I hope you remember me from the Captain's cocktail party. Ted Cavanaugh," he said, extending his hand. "After all that talking, your throat must be dry. Why don't we have a glass of wine or a cocktail?"

Celia's first instinct was to refuse, but she hesitated. She definitely did not look forward to being alone with the constant weight of her thoughts. And the weight of the necklace, she added silently.

"That would be nice," she answered.

"The Regency Bar is nearest. Why don't we try it?"

"Sounds fine to me."

A few minutes later the waiter was placing their drinks on the table. Chardonnay for Celia, vodka on the rocks for Ted.

Ted followed his plan to stay away from raising the topic of Lady Em's death or the Cleopatra necklace. Instead he asked, "Celia, you must have done a lot of studying to become such a knowledgeable gemologist. Is there a special kind of school that you attended?"

It was an easy question on a safe topic. "I went to England after college and became a fellow at the Gemological Institute of Great Britain. But as one of the professors said, 'It takes a lifetime to become a master gemologist.' "

"How did you become interested in that as a career?"

Ted did not miss the troubled expression on Celia's face. Celia was recalling that she had had a similar conversation with Professor Longworth only a few days ago, about how she got started in the jewelry business. Was it only *a few* days? She recalled being uncomfortable then, but for whatever reason she felt comfortable talking to Ted Cavanaugh.

"My father was a gemologist. When I was little, I loved to put jewelry, fake of course, on my dolls. He began to teach me the difference between the fakes and the really good stuff, and how to use a loupe." Then she added, "He died two years ago. He left me two hundred fifty thousand dollars, which I lost in a scam."

She looked directly at him. "I read about what happened to you," Ted admitted.

"Then you know that a lot of people think I was in on the fraud and I helped cheat them out of their hard-earned money."

"I read the account your ex-fiancé gave to *People* magazine—"

"It's a total lie!" Celia said heatedly.

Ted considered, then responded. "If it's any consolation, I simply can't envision you as a thief. Or a murderer." Why am I making a statement like that? he asked himself. Because it's true, he thought.

"Why would he do this to me?"

"I think the obvious first reason is revenge that you didn't stick by him. The second obvious reason is that he's looking for a better plea deal from the U.S. Attorney's Office. He basically confessed in the article, but he knows they already have the evidence to convict him. He's telling them that you were involved and he'll cooperate with them against you. I really think that's what's going on."

"But I was a victim too," Celia protested.

"I know that, Celia, I know that."

He went back to a safe subject. "You said that your father was a gemologist and that he died two years ago. How about your mother?"

"She died when I was a baby."

"Brothers? Sisters?"

"None. My father never remarried. And can you believe I'm angry at him that he didn't? I would love to have brothers and sisters."

Ted thought of his own background. His mother and father were still in great shape, and they and his two brothers were a frequent presence in his life. "I'm sure you have a lot of good friends?"

Celia shook her head. "I used to. I'm afraid I lost some very good friends, the ones who invested in Steven's fund."

"Surely they don't blame you?"

"I introduced them to Steven and he has a golden tongue. That doesn't make me very popular with them. My friends weren't wealthy. It really hurt them when they lost their money."

I'll bet that it hurt you too, Ted thought, but didn't voice the opinion. Instead he leaned back, took a sip of his drink, looked at Celia. He was sure to his very soul that she was innocent of Lady Em's murder and that she was not a thief. Her eyes are so sad, he thought. She's been through so much.

68

Brenda attended Celia's presentation and admitted to herself that Celia was very knowledgeable about gems. She had been getting close to Lady Em, Brenda thought. I wouldn't be surprised if Lady Em had asked her to take a close look at the picnic bracelet. But even if she did, it would be Celia's word against mine, she reassured herself. And certainly with her fiancé implicating her in a crime, I'll bet they won't believe a word Celia says.

Ralphie had emailed to express his sorrow regarding Lady Em's passing. Wisely, he had not included any mention of Lady Em's jewelry.

Brenda made her way upstairs, smiling particularly at people whose faces she recognized. A number of them had offered condolences, recognizing that she had been Lady Em's assistant for many years. When she reached her room, she went directly to the phone and called Ralph.

When he answered, she started by saying, "Don't say too much. You never know if these conversations are being recorded."

"I understand," he replied. "How are you, honey?"

Brenda blushed. It was so nice after all these years to have someone call her "honey." Even her mother had not been given to voicing any endearments.

"I'm good, sweetie," she promised, "although, of course, I'm heartsick about Lady Em's death. But it does mean that I'm free of the responsibility of being at her beck and call. So if you still want me to marry you, I'll be home this Sunday."

"Of course, I'll be waiting for you," Ralph said. "I've been wanting to be married to you since the first day we met. I promise you now that Lady Em is gone, things are going to be very different."

"Yes, they will be," Brenda agreed. "Your buttercup says good-bye for now, my Ralphie. Kisses."

She hung up the phone smiling. I wonder how long it will be before I get the three hundred thousand from the estate. It wouldn't have killed her to leave me half a million, or even a million bucks, she thought. I deserve it.

Satisfied with her self-justification, Brenda picked up the book she had been intending to start. She walked over and opened the door to the balcony. It was much too windy to go out. She was itching for this voyage to be over so she could get back to New York.

Brenda could feel Ralphie's arms around her as she began to read the tender passages in Jane Eyre's journey from tragedy after tragedy to reconciliation with Mr. Rochester. He reminds me of Ralphie, she thought, as the picture evolved in her mind of the towering figure who was Jane Eyre's hero. She settled back in the club chair and began to read again.

69

Devon Michaelson attended the session with Celia and the entertainment director but only half listened to both the questions and responses. He was still seething from his meeting with Gregory Morrison and the ship owner's obnoxious follow-up phone call minutes later.

"You're from Interpol, right?" Morrison had asked.

"Yes, I am."

"And you're on this ship specifically to safeguard the Cleopatra necklace?"

"That is true."

"Well, I must say you've done a lousy job. Our most prominent passenger has been murdered and the necklace has been stolen. And it's obvious you've made no progress finding the Man with One Thousand Faces. All this time you were busy throwing ashes over the side of my ship. If you were my employee, I'd fire you."

"Fortunately, I am not your employee, Mr. Morrison. I work for the best international detective agency in the world. And I might add that under no circumstances would I ever consider working for you."

When the jewelry presentation was finished, Devon lingered

near the door long enough to see Celia leave with Ted Cavanaugh. A romance in the making? he wondered. I don't care one way or the other. There are less than two days left on the cruise. Before we reach Southampton, I intend to find that necklace. And I'd love to shove it down Morrison's throat, he thought.

70

Professor Henry Longworth had not intended to go to Celia's third presentation, however after his lecture was finished and he had had a quick lunch, he decided to go. He got to the auditorium just a few minutes before Celia was introduced and stayed at the back until just before the program was set to begin.

When he saw Brenda come in, he shrank against the wall. The last thing he needed was to be subjected to her tiresome comments during the jewelry discussion. He waited until she had settled into a seat before he circumnavigated and took a seat as far away as humanly possible.

When he sat down, he took a good look around. To his chagrin, Celia had almost twice the audience he had had for his talk. She's talking about jewelry, base baubles, he thought. I'm talking about the Bard, the finest writer the world has ever known!

Jealous? I admit I am, he told himself. Nevertheless, she is a rather nice young woman. Is she poor Cordelia, falsely accused and misunderstood, or is she Lady Macbeth, a cold killer encased in lovely femininity? he mused.

He recognized that he was engaging in his favorite dalliance, trying to decide if anyone would guess who murdered Lady Em.

By the end of Celia's lecture, he was sure no one would suspect her. Then who *would* people suspect?

He looked around. How about Brenda Martin? There she was, sitting five rows ahead of him and far to his left. He thought of how she had bolted up from the table after the Captain's announcement that Lady Haywood had died in her sleep. But then she had returned only a few minutes later. It was obvious that what should have been distressing news, that her employer had died, had not affected her appetite. To his disappointment she did not discuss what had happened when she reached the suite. Of course, by then speculation was widely available on news sites that Lady Em had been murdered and her famous necklace stolen.

He glanced over at Brenda inadvertently and caught her eye. I'd love to read your mind, he thought. I wonder what I'd find there. *False face must hide what the false heart doth know.*

When the hour ended, he stood up with the others, waited until Brenda had left the auditorium, then sauntered out with the few remaining guests. He did not feel any need for company and went directly to his suite. There he opened the bar and made himself a gin martini. With a sigh of satisfaction, he settled in the club chair, put his feet on the hassock, and began to sip.

This trip may be crazy, he thought, but even so it does have all the amenities they promised. And a murder on board is such an interesting plot twist. He began to laugh.

71

When she left Ted Cavanaugh, Celia went straight to her room. She admitted to herself that she had really enjoyed sharing a cocktail with him, but did not want to dwell on it. Instead she was desperate to know what people really thought of her.

She had spotted Yvonne and her two friends in the audience. She could only imagine how Yvonne was feeling. I hope my presentation took her mind off things for a while, Celia thought. She had barely reached the suite when the phone rang. She hoped it was Alvirah, and she was pleased to hear her voice.

"Celia, your presentation was simply wonderful," Alvirah said. "I thought you were terrific the other day, but you were even better today."

Take refuge my heart, Celia thought to herself. But she had to admit Alvirah's compliment made her feel much better.

"I've been giving a lot of thought to your situation," Alvirah continued. "I'd like to come see you in your room."

"I could use a friend. Come on over."

She was so used to seeing Alvirah and Willy together that it was a surprise to see Alvirah alone at her door. When she let her in, Alvirah anxiously asked, "Are you sure this isn't an intrusion? I know you might be tired after your presentation."

"Frankly, I'm glad to have your company, Alvirah. When I'm alone, I have too much time to think."

"Well, that makes me feel better," Alvirah said, as she sat on the couch.

"Celia, Willy and I know perfectly well that there is no way on God's earth that you ever would or could have harmed Lady Emily or stolen her necklace."

"Thank you," Celia murmured. Should I? she asked herself. She decided the answer was yes.

She reached into her pocket and took out the Cleopatra necklace. Seeing the shocked expression on Alvirah's face, she said, "I didn't steal it. Lady Em gave it to me. Let me explain what happened.

"Right after I got back to my suite last night, Lady Em phoned and asked me to come to her suite. She told me to bring my loupe, the eyepiece I use to examine jewelry. When I got to her suite, she handed me a bracelet and asked for my opinion regarding how valuable it was. It was easy to see that it was composed of inferior diamonds. It was virtually worthless. When I told Lady Em, she looked terribly sad. She told me that she believed her assistant Brenda had been switching her good jewelry for cheap imitations.

" 'But Brenda has been with you for twenty years,' I said. Lady Em told me that she was very sure of what she was saying, and that Brenda looked extremely uncomfortable when Lady Em told her the jewelry didn't look right.

"Then she said that she felt so disappointed because she had always been so kind to Brenda and very generous."

"How sad," Alvirah sighed.

"That isn't all," Celia continued. "Lady Em also told me that she was convinced that Roger Pearson was cheating her. Apparently she told him yesterday that she was planning to have an outside accountant go over all of her affairs, and he looked very distressed."

"I can understand that," Alvirah said. "Willy and I heard him shouting at Yvonne the other night when we walked past their suite. He was saying that he could go to prison for twenty years."

"Alvirah, what do I do about the necklace? Lady Em told me she had decided to do what Ted Cavanaugh asked. When she returned to New York, she would give the necklace to her lawyers and they would turn it over to Ted. Apparently at the cocktail party, the Captain had suggested to Lady Em that she give it to him to keep in his private safe. Last night Lady Em gave it to me and asked me to bring it to the Captain this morning." Celia shook her head. "I've been so afraid to tell anyone that I have it. I'm sure there are plenty of people who already think I'm a thief because of the hedge fund. It will be easy for them to believe that I killed Lady Em and stole the necklace."

"You're right," Alvirah agreed. "But you can't be walking around with it in your pocket. And it will look terrible for you if someone finds it in your suite."

"That's my point," Celia sighed. "I'm in trouble if I admit having it, and I'm in trouble if I hold on to it."

"Celia, do you want me to hold it for you? I'll give it to Willy. Let him be the one carrying it around. It will be safe with him. I can guarantee you that."

"But what happens when we reach Southampton?" Celia asked. "What will you and Willy do with it then?"

"I have a little time to figure that out," Alvirah said grimly. "I'm considered a pretty good detective. Let's see if I can solve this case before we reach Southampton."

With a sense of being unburdened, Celia picked up the necklace and handed it to Alvirah.

"It is so beautiful," Alvirah commented, as she put it in her pocketbook.

"It is," Celia agreed. "I think it is the most beautiful piece of jewelry I have ever seen."

Alvirah paused, looked at Celia and asked with a smile, "Should I be worried about the Cleopatra curse?"

"No," Celia said, smiling back at her. "The curse is that 'whoever *takes* this necklace to sea, will never live to reach the shore.' And if the curse was real, poor Lady Em was the victim."

As she spoke, Celia's mind was filled with the memory of Lady Em's troubled, sad face when she told her that her two trusted confidants, Brenda and Roger, had been cheating her.

72

Raymond Broad, Lady Em's butler on the ship, had been sure that the information he sent to the gossip website PMT about Lady Em's murder and the stolen necklace would be traced to him. To his surprise, he was not questioned beyond his original statement that he had found Lady Em dead in her suite. The security chief called to admonish him to not speak to guests or anyone else about what he saw in Lady Em's room. But they appeared now to be assigning the blame for tipping off the news media to a mysterious jewel thief who was purportedly on the ship.

His thoughts returned to when he was in the suite and realized Lady Em was dead. A few feet from her bed the door of her wall safe was open and jewelry was scattered on the floor. He regretted that he had not followed his first impulse. Take some of the jewelry. Maybe take all of it. It would be assumed that whoever killed her and opened the safe would have taken it. He had even considered hiding it in the breakfast cart which he wheeled away after being dismissed by Dr. Blake.

But what if they had treated him like a suspect? Would they have searched him or the breakfast cart? Kicking himself, he realized that if he had merely closed the door of the safe, no one would have focused on a robbery. He could have left with the jewelry and no one would have been the wiser.

His other reason for regret was that Lady Em was known as a very big tipper. So on all counts I lose, he decided.

After Lady Em's suite was sealed, he had been reassigned and was now in charge of both Professor Longworth's and Brenda Martin's cabins. He did not think much of either of them. The professor barely acknowledged him when he was in the room. And Brenda Martin was constantly asking for one thing after another.

Broad had received a call from his contact at PMT confirming payment to him for his tip about Lady Em and asking him to be very sure to notify them immediately of any further developments on the murder and the theft. Raymond had eagerly assented, even while he admitted to himself that it was unlikely he would uncover any new information before *Queen Charlotte* arrived in Southampton.

The phone in his little kitchen rang. It was Brenda Martin. She wanted afternoon tea served in her suite. It was not necessary for her to add that she wanted the tiny sandwiches and pastries that were always served with afternoon tea. There won't be a crumb left when she's finished, Raymond thought.

73

The Man with One Thousand Faces had narrowed down the number of suspects who might have taken the necklace to only one, Brenda Martin. He knew she had a key to Lady Em's suite. What would be more natural than for her to go there, ostensibly to check on Lady Haywood? It had been obvious that Lady Em was not feeling well when she got up from her final dinner.

As he straightened his tie and started down to dinner, he wondered what he would say to Brenda if he saw her. He was tempted to say, "Brenda, have a good meal. It may very well be your last supper."

74

Roger did not realize his arms had stopped flailing. He did not hear a voice shouting, "Grab him, he's sinking!" He did not feel arms go under both his shoulders. He was not aware that he was being pulled up and lifted onto something.

He did not feel a blanket being thrown over him. He was unaware of the sound of an engine starting to roar or that he was being lifted up and hoisted over a railing. In his mind he was beginning to sink. The waves breaking over him were making it impossible to breathe.

He could barely hear the ship's doctor say, "Take him down to the infirmary. We've got to warm him up."

On those comforting words, Roger drifted off to sleep.

75

Alvirah held her pocketbook tight after she left Celia and went back to her room. Willy was there and looked up expectantly. He was surprised that Alvirah, before she even greeted him, turned around and bolted the door of the suite.

"What's that about?" Willy asked.

"Let me show you what it's about," she whispered. "And keep your voice down."

Opening her pocketbook, she reached into it and pulled out the Cleopatra necklace.

"Is that what I think it is?" he asked as he took the three-strand necklace from her hand.

"Yes, it is," Alvirah answered.

"Where did you get it?"

"Celia gave it to me."

"How did she get it? Don't tell me she was the one who smothered that poor old woman."

"Willy, you know as well as I do that Celia Kilbride is no murderer or thief. This is what happened."

Her voice still low, she told Willy everything Celia had shared with her. She finished by saying, "You can understand how frightened she is. She was absolutely certain that if people found out she had the necklace, they would never believe that Lady Em gave it to her."

"I can see that," Willy agreed. "So what do we do now? I don't want anyone to find out you have it and end up killing you."

"You're right, Willy, and that's why *you* have to hold on to it, keep it with you at all times. It will be safest with you."

"But after we get off the ship, what do we do with it?" Willy asked.

"Celia told me that Lady Em was planning to give it to Ted Cavanaugh because she agreed with him that it belonged to the people of Egypt."

"Well, I just hope they don't frisk me," Willy said, matter-of-factly.

He stood up and slid the necklace into his pants pocket, where it immediately caused a visible bulge. Alvirah saw the look of dismay on his face.

"When you put your jacket on, nobody will notice," she said.

"I hope not." After a pause, Willy asked, "Okay, what do we do now?"

"Willy, you know I'm a good detective."

He looked alarmed. "Don't tell me you're going to try to solve this mystery. Don't forget. You're dealing with a killer who didn't get what he or she wanted."

"I understand that. But when you think about it, Lady Em told Celia that she was sure both Roger Pearson and Brenda were cheating her. Isn't that awful?"

"We heard Roger and Yvonne at each other's throats the other night. It's a heck of a coincidence that Roger was dead less than twenty-four hours later."

"I know it is. And Lady Em was dead only hours after she told Celia that Brenda had been switching her jewelry." She continued, "You know, Willy, I've been wondering if Roger Pearson fell overboard or if he got a little help from Yvonne."

"You don't think she pushed him over, do you?" Willy asked incredulously.

"I'm not saying it, but I'm thinking it, just wondering about it. I mean you can certainly see that those two were not close. She was at Celia's lecture today with a couple of friends. She sure didn't look to me like a grieving widow. And when you think about it, with Lady Em dead and Roger dead, the question about what he was doing with her finances will probably just go away. And that is very good news for Yvonne."

They stared at each other. Willy spoke first. "Do you think Yvonne might have also killed Lady Em?"

"I wouldn't be surprised."

"But what about this rumor about a jewel thief, 'the Man with One Thousand Faces'?"

"I don't know. I just don't know," Alvirah said, lost in thought.

76

One by one, people gathered for a formal dinner. At one table were Professor Longworth, Yvonne, Celia and Brenda. At the table next to theirs Alvirah and Willy, Devon Michaelson, Ted Cavanaugh and Anna DeMille were seated. Conversation at both tables was limited and awkward.

"Acupuncture is wonderful," Alvirah was telling Cavanaugh. "I don't know what I'd do without it. Sometimes when I fall asleep, I dream I'm having those little needles stuck in me. And I always wake up feeling better."

"I can understand that," Ted told her. "My mother goes for acupuncture to her arthritic hip, and she says it does her a world of good."

"Oh, your mother has arthritis?" Alvirah exclaimed. "Is she Irish?"

"Her maiden name was Maureen Byrnes. And my father is half-Irish."

"The reason I ask," Alvirah said, "is that arthritis is believed to be an Irish disease. My theory is that our Irish ancestors were out in the cold and the rain gathering peat for their fires. The dampness seeped into their DNA."

Ted laughed. He acknowledged to himself that he found Alvirah both interesting and refreshing.

Anna DeMille did not like to be left out of a conversation for long. "I saw you had a drink with Celia Kilbride," she told Ted, "and you attended her presentation. I think she's a very good speaker, don't you?"

"Yes, I do," Ted said quietly.

Willy listened to the conversation as his hand went restlessly to his pocket where the Cleopatra necklace was being kept. He was glad not to get into the discussion about acupuncture. Alvirah was always urging him to get it for his back pain. And it was uncomfortable to hear that an obviously smart guy like Ted Cavanaugh had a relative who used it.

Devon Michaelson had been listening with little interest, but then he saw Gregory Morrison walking about, visiting from table to table. Probably telling everybody they have nothing to worry about, he thought.

His attention shifted to the table nearest them. There were only four people there now. He could see that the conversation was stilted. None of them looked happy to be there. Then he noticed that Morrison was on his way to Longworth's table. He bristled at the sight of him, then acknowledged to himself that he did not easily accept criticism.

Devon strained to hear what was being said, but he could barely pick up a word. An additional diversion was the fact that Anna DeMille had placed her hand over his and was asking him in a tender voice, "Are you feeling better today, Devon dear?"

Gregory Morrison was fully aware that the chairs had been spaced farther apart to make it less obvious that two people were missing from the table he was approaching. Lady Haywood and Roger Pearson, the jerk who had fallen overboard. Neither was a great loss to the human race as far as he was concerned. It seemed appropriate, however, to offer his sympathy to Pearson's widow, who hardly looked devastated by her loss. He knew crocodile tears when he saw them. He took comfort from the fact that his ship could not be held responsible for the loss of someone who had been stupid enough to sit on the railing. After a few words to Yvonne, he put his hand on Brenda's shoulder. "I understand that you were Lady Haywood's trusted companion of twenty years," he said. And I wonder if you killed her, he added silently to himself.

Brenda's eyes became moist. "They were the best twenty years of my life," she said simply. "I'll miss her forever."

She must have been left some money by Lady Haywood, Morrison thought. I wonder how much.

"Mr. Morrison," Brenda said, "in addition to the missing Cleopatra necklace, Lady Em brought a lot of expensive jewelry on this cruise. My understanding is that it was on the floor near her bed when they found her. Are you taking steps to assure that nothing happens to it?"

"I am sure that the Captain and our security chief are following all appropriate procedures."

Morrison turned away from the table. He saw that Devon Michaelson, Interpol's Dick Tracy, was at the next table, and steered around it. He spread his charm at other tables, then went back to his seat next to the Captain.

"They all appear to have gotten over the unfortunate incidents," he told Fairfax, then turned his attention to the smoked salmon on the plate in front of him.

77

Though Professor Longworth found Brenda boring, he would not have been happy to know that his opinion was reciprocated. She considered him an absolute dud. *If those eyebrows go up one more time, I will throw my dessert at him,* she thought. Without waiting for that to happen, she ate the warm apple pie and vanilla topping as quickly as possible. She finished half the cup of coffee and then got up. All she wanted to do was to talk to Ralphie. She looked at her watch. *It's eight-thirty now. That means it's four-thirty or five-thirty in New York. A good time to call.*

Brenda had a funny feeling when she entered her suite. She looked carefully around, but it was obvious that it was empty. *I'll call Raymond and tell him I want another slice of pie,* she thought, and another cup of coffee. She placed the call and told him, "Make it about ten minutes." She disconnected and phoned Ralphie.

Brenda had no way of knowing that Ralphie was fully packed and ready to leave. Neither did she know that he had just finished transferring all the hard-earned stolen money from their joint account into an account in his name.

The phone rang three times before he picked it up. His bark, "Hello," for whatever reason did not sound endearing.

"Ralphie, it's your buttercup," she cooed.

"Oh, I was hoping it was you," he said, his tone now warm and loving.

"I miss you so much," Brenda sighed, "but I'll be home in three days. And I'm planning a surprise for when I see you. I bought it at the jewelry store on the main level."

"I can hardly wait," Ralphie said sincerely. "That means I should have a surprise for you."

"Oh, that is so sweet," Brenda gushed. "I'm counting the hours until I see you. Good-bye, my dear Ralphie. Kisses."

"Good-bye, my buttercup," Ralphie said, and disconnected the phone.

Well, that does it for the buttercup, he thought, as he snapped shut his third suitcase.

He glanced at his watch. He was meeting his new girlfriend—not really new, but at least now they wouldn't have to sneak around any-more. They were taking a 10 P.M. Amtrak sleeper train to Chicago. But before he left, he took a long look around the apartment. Very comfortable, he thought. In a way I hate to leave.

He laughed out loud.

Poor dear Brenda, if she turns *me* in, she'll end up in the cell right next to mine.

Lulu's apartment was on the main floor of the same building. It wasn't hers; she had been subletting month to month. They had agreed to meet at Grand Central Station rather than leave the build-ing together. He wasn't sure how long he would hang on to Lulu. But for the moment, she would be a breath of fresh air after five years with klutzy "buttercup."

78

As Raymond Broad was passing the room, he could hear Brenda's voice on the phone. He leaned his ear to the door as she said, "Good-bye, my dear Ralphie. Kisses." She then made several smooching sounds with her lips.

She has a boyfriend, he thought. I would never have guessed.

Before he knocked on the door, he lifted the coverlet to make sure the kitchen had sent the right flavor pie. Brenda had scolded him once before for bringing pecan pie, claiming she had an allergy to nuts. "Rubbish," he said to himself as he saw that the kitchen had made the same error again. He hurried back to switch pies.

In her room Brenda had a weird sense of something wrong. And then she felt some type of cloth being pulled over her head and something being tightened around her throat. An instant later she felt herself being tossed down into what she believed was the closet.

Don't panic, she warned herself. Don't let him know you can still breathe. With all her will she held her breath until she heard the door of the closet close, then began to inhale and exhale as quietly as she could. With each successive breath, her breathing became more normal. Although something very tight had been pulled around her neck, she had managed to slip a finger inside it, leaving her throat open just enough to breathe.

The Man with One Thousand Faces was sure that no one had

seen him come down the corridor and into the room. Working swiftly, he emptied Brenda's purse on the floor, then rushed to the safe. No necklace there either, he observed. Then he rifled through the suitcases and dresser. "I'd have sworn she was the one who had it," he grumbled, as he opened the cabin door an inch and saw that the coast was clear. Walking swiftly but at the same time trying to appear casual, he quickly covered the distance back to his own room.

Less than two minutes later Raymond returned to Brenda's room and tapped on the door. Hearing nothing, he opened the door and went in. He was surprised to see that there was no one there. He placed the coffee and dessert on the cocktail table. But then he heard the sound of someone grunting and kicking in the closet. Not sure that he was hearing correctly, he walked slowly to the door and opened it. He was greeted by the sight of Brenda sprawled on the floor, one hand over her pillowcase-covered head and the other on her throat.

Raymond scrambled to the dresser for a pair of scissors. He rushed back, knelt down and said, "I have you. Let go of the rope." Slipping his finger into where Brenda's had been, he carefully slid one blade of the scissors between her neck and the rope. A moment after he applied pressure the cord snapped. He used the scissors to cut away the pillowcase and ripped it away from her face.

She breathed in life-giving air. He waited a few minutes until she began to caress her throat with her hands. He helped her to a sitting position and then dragged her to her feet.

"What took you so long?" she gasped. "I could have been choked to death!"

"Miss Brenda," he said, "let's get you into your chair. A cup of coffee will help you get settled."

Leaning over him, Brenda collapsed in a chair and reached for the coffee.

Raymond picked up the phone and called the chief of security to report an "incident" that had occurred in Brenda's room. Saunders promised to come right over and bring Dr. Blake with him.

Turning back to Brenda, Raymond said, "Is there anything I can do—"

She cut him off. "Go get me a towel with some ice cubes in it. I want to wrap it around my neck."

"Ma'am, I think it would be a good idea if I stayed with you until—"

"I SAID GET ME A COLD TOWEL!"

"Right away, ma'am," Raymond said, delighted to have a reason to leave the suite.

Before Raymond left, Brenda called out to him, "Tell the Captain someone tried to strangle me, and I insist on getting better protection until we reach Southampton."

Too bad that her dear Ralphie isn't around, Raymond thought as he tiptoed out. He went directly to a storage closet and closed the door behind him. As soon as the connection was established, he whispered, "Another attempted murder. This time Lady Haywood's personal assistant Brenda Martin was the intended victim. He tried to strangle her, but she managed to slip a finger under the cord and keep breathing. She didn't talk about anything missing from her room, so the motive is not clear."

Raymond slipped the cell phone back into his pocket and exited the storage closet.

One minute later his phone registered that he had received a text. It was from John Saunders, the chief of security. He was being summoned back to Brenda's suite, where the Captain and the ship owner were waiting for him. With a towel and ice bucket in hand, Raymond hurried back to her cabin.

Brenda was still in the armchair where he had left her. Raymond's first glance revealed that she had finished the vanilla ice cream, the apple pie and the coffee in the few minutes she had been alone. But there was no missing that she had an ugly red bruise all around her neck. She could have been asphyxiated, he thought, but the first thing he heard her say to Dr. Blake was that she wouldn't be alive if Raymond hadn't rescued her. She added that she planned to sue the cruise line because even though they knew there was a murderer on board, they had not taken the trouble to secure the halls from a serial killer.

Captain Fairfax began a lengthy apology, but he was cut off by Gregory Morrison. The ship owner assured Brenda that he would take good care of her if she would agree to not say a word to the other passengers about what happened to her.

"Whether or not I say a word won't matter to what you are going to pay me," Brenda gasped as she ran her fingers over her sore neck. "I could be dead," she moaned, "and it would be because all of you failed in your duty to protect us. The next thing you know is we'll all be on the deck singing, 'Nearer, my God, to thee, nearer to thee.'"

79

Five hundred nautical miles away the *Paradise* ship's doctor was anxiously studying his new patient. He didn't even know his name. No ID had been found in what little clothing he still had on when they pulled him from the water.

The man was suffering from hypothermia and pneumonitis. The few words he had uttered were almost incomprehensible: "pushed me, get her" were repeated several times. But with a temperature of one hundred four, the doctor attributed them to delirious rants.

He looked up as the door opened and the ship's captain came into the room. The Captain did not waste time on pleasantries. "How is he?" he asked brusquely as he studied the unexpected passenger who had been brought aboard ten hours earlier.

"I don't know, sir," the doctor answered, his tone as always deferential to the Captain. "He is stabilized, but his breathing is very labored. He's not out of the woods yet, but I believe he's going to make it."

"Considering how cold it is in these waters, I'm surprised he was able to survive. Then again, we don't know how long he was in the water," the Captain observed.

"No, we don't, sir. But he had two things in his favor. In the medical community we often joke that the person who's best-suited for cold is fit and fat. His ample fat likely insulated his body's core, making him less susceptible to hypothermia. But he has the muscular shoulders and legs of a swimmer. When he was treading water, those muscles would have generated heat, offering additional protection from the cold."

The Captain was silent for a moment, and then snapped, "Well, do your best and keep me posted. Did he give his name yet?"

"No, sir, he has not." The doctor did not add that the patient was mumbling about being "pushed." He knew the Captain preferred hard facts over speculation. He was sure that those utterings would turn out to be hypothermia-induced delusions when and if the patient recovered.

"Do you expect him to pull through?" the captain asked.

"I do, sir, and I won't leave him until I'm sure he is out of danger."

"How long do you expect that to be?"

"We'll know more over the next seven hours, sir."

"Notify me immediately if he regains consciousness." The Captain left the room. Immediately the ship's doctor pulled a reclining chair over to the side of the bed, leaned back in it and pulled a blanket around his neck.

Sweet dreams, Mr. Mystery Guest, he thought, as he closed his eyes and drifted into a sound sleep.

Day Five

80

Alvirah and Willy, Devon Michaelson, Anna DeMille and Ted Cavanaugh gathered for a quiet breakfast, which turned out to be anything but.

A few minutes after they sat down, Brenda arrived at her table. Yvonne and Professor Longworth were already there. Brenda in her newfound glory, with a red mark from the choking around her neck, had originally planned to have breakfast in her suite. After confirming that she was not seriously injured, Dr. Blake urged her to spend the night in the infirmary. She refused, preferring the privacy of her cabin.

She decided it would be much more interesting to share her near death experience with her fellow passengers in the Queen's Lounge. She made a point of stroking her neck as she sat down, and then made an audible groan as she swallowed a glass of fresh orange juice. At their exclamations of "What happened to you?" she was happy to tell her table mates the story without sparing a single detail.

"Are you sure you didn't see the person who assaulted you?" Yvonne asked nervously.

"He must have been hiding in the closet. When I was turned the other way, he attacked me from behind," Brenda said, holding her hand to her chest at the memory.

"Did you notice anything that might help them figure out who attacked you?" Yvonne asked.

Brenda shook her head. "Not really. Whoever it was, was very strong," she said.

She doesn't have a clue, Longworth thought. Very interesting.

Brenda continued. "Whatever he put around my neck, he was going to use it to strangle me. I began to black out. I remember being pushed into the closet. I was fortunate that I had managed to get a finger inside the noose before he started pulling. I struggled at first, but then I decided it would be better to pretend I was blacking out. I was right on the edge of losing consciousness when I felt his grip start to loosen."

"Oh my God," Yvonne said.

"Oh my God is right," Brenda reiterated. "My life started to pass before my—"

Now it was Longworth's turn to say, "Oh my God—when will this end? Are we *all* in danger?"

Brenda continued. "But I lay still, barely breathing. He was in my room for a time, doing who knows what. I listened until I heard the sound of the cabin door open and close and whoever did it left."

By now Yvonne appeared as breathless as Brenda. "What a horrible experience," she moaned. "Hearing about you struggling to breathe makes me realize how awful it must have been for my darling Roger."

To Longworth Brenda looked clearly annoyed that the focus on her fifteen minutes of fame was momentarily shared by another person's misfortune.

Brenda continued. "To make a long story short—"

Way too late for that, Longworth sighed to himself.

"I survived, and I am alive to tell the tale. And it wasn't until this morning that on top of everything else, I realized my very valuable necklace is missing."

Sensing she had lost her audience, Brenda finished eating quickly, walked over to the next table, sat down and began massaging the bruises on her neck.

She appeared delighted that Alvirah and Willy and Ted Cavanaugh were particularly concerned as she recounted her harrowing adventure. On the other hand Anna DeMille sighed, "In a way I'm jealous of you. I could just imagine being in that circumstance." She turned to Devon and put her hand on his arm. "I would hope that you would be the one to rescue me," she said sweetly.

Ted stayed only a few minutes before excusing himself. That was when he murmured to Alvirah, "I have to call a client in France, but then I want to check on Celia."

"Good idea," Alvirah confirmed.

A few minutes later Brenda glanced around and spotted Yvonne's Hamptons friends. Massaging her neck and wincing as she walked, she headed directly for their table.

Alvirah swallowed her last gulp of coffee and said, "Willy, let's take a walk on the deck."

Willy looked out the window. "It's pouring, honey," he said.

Alvirah followed his glance. "Oh, it is. You're right. Let's go upstairs instead. I want to phone and check on Celia."

81

Celia had slept mercifully well after dinner, no longer carrying the Cleopatra necklace and having confided in Alvirah had taken a weight off her shoulders. But when she had opened her eyes at six-thirty in the morning, she realized there was something else. She had thoroughly enjoyed talking to Ted Cavanaugh. She knew that he was being genuine when he told her that he believed she had nothing to do with Lady Em's death. She wished she had told him what Lady Em had said about Brenda and Roger but decided that might have made him wonder why she knew so much.

After replaying their conversation in her mind, she turned her attention to the nagging question of why she had let herself be swept off her feet by Steven. Why hadn't she been more careful? A little checking would have quickly revealed that much of what he was telling her was not true. She wondered if it was her father's fault for dying so young, and leaving her in such a vulnerable state. But at that thought she was embarrassed and angry that she could even consider blaming him. "I love you, Daddy," she whispered as healing tears rushed to her eyes. "I have only myself to blame."

She sat up, reached for a robe and phoned for coffee and a muffin.

I won't let this happen again, she thought. I have to be sure. She went over to the table and opened her laptop. Celia didn't remember the name of Ted's law firm, so she went to Google and typed in Ted Cavanaugh, NYC lawyer. A website for the Boswell, Bitzer and Cavanaugh firm was one of the links. She clicked on it, and the site came up. She clicked on Our People, and when Ted's picture appeared, she scanned the brief bio below it. Celia heaved a sigh of relief. Ted is exactly who he said he is.

Minutes later her phone rang. It was Alvirah.

"Celia, I just wanted to say, be careful," Alvirah warned. "Brenda Martin just came down to breakfast. She said someone tried to strangle her and that she would have died if the butler hadn't entered her room before she choked to death."

"Oh, poor Brenda," Celia sighed, even as she remembered that Lady Em had told her that Brenda was a thief.

"My worry is that the thief may be searching for the Cleopatra necklace," Alvirah continued. "So you must be very careful over the next two days. And be careful when you're walking. The ship is starting to roll from side to side. If you haven't been outside yet, you might not know that we're having a terrible rainstorm."

"I haven't," Celia answered. "Alvirah, I'm worried I might have put you and Willy in danger."

"Oh, we'll be okay," Alvirah said confidently. "No one is going to kill me while Willy's around, and I don't think anyone is going to tangle with Willy."

"That makes me feel better," Celia said, "but please be careful."

"We will be," Alvirah promised.

Celia had barely hung up the phone when it rang again. It was Ted Cavanaugh. His voice was solicitous. "Celia, you didn't come down to breakfast. Are you all right?"

"I'm fine," Celia assured him. "I slept late this morning, which is the first time I've done that in recent memory."

"I'm calling to warn you to be careful," Ted said. "Brenda was almost murdered last night. She said someone attacked her in her room and tried to strangle her. She was robbed of a very valuable pearl necklace."

Celia did not say that Alvirah had just called her. She also didn't tell Ted that the only necklace she had seen Brenda wearing was of very poor quality. Unless the necklace she claims was stolen was one of Lady Em's. But she kept that thought to herself.

"Celia, my office just sent me material for a brief I have to finish tonight. Let's have lunch tomorrow."

"I'd like that," Celia said simply.

"Good. How about one o'clock in the tearoom on your deck?"

"That will be fine," Celia confirmed, then held on to the phone for a moment after Ted disconnected. "I don't feel all by myself, alone, right now," she said aloud, as she hung up the phone and picked up her coffee cup.

82

Gregory Morrison watched as Captain Fairfax and his chief security officer entered his room. He looked at them and past them. "Where's Inspector Clouseau from Interpol?" he demanded. "I said I wanted him here as well."

"I asked Mr. Michaelson to join us," Captain Fairfax said nervously. "But he told me he had absolutely no intention of coming here to be humiliated by you."

"You weren't supposed to ask him to come. I told you to tell him to come." Morrison sighed. "Forget it, he's useless anyhow."

Morrison paced around his suite as he spoke. "That cow Brenda Martin is running all over the dining room showing her swollen neck to anyone who will give her the time of day. Don't you people realize that all the passengers will be afraid of being in their rooms alone?"

He looked John Saunders squarely in the eye. "Can you give me any good reason why I should keep paying you? After a passenger is murdered and her jewelry stolen, why didn't it occur to you to have someone in the hallway to stand guard?"

Saunders had taught himself to overlook Morrison's constant jibes. "May I remind you, Mr. Morrison, we agreed to try to keep things on board as normal as possible. Armed guards in the hallways outside the passengers' suites is not normal. I specifically recall your saying that we are not running a prison."

"I suppose you're right," Morrison said grudgingly.

Captain Fairfax took over. "Frankly, Mr. Morrison," he said firmly, "we should be focusing on how we are going to respond to this latest," he paused, "incident. It had not been picked up by the news sites before I came up here, but—"

Morrison rummaged in his pocket and found his phone. He tapped in the name of the ship. "Just what I was afraid of," he snarled. "The first headline is 'Another Passenger Attacked on *Queen Charlotte*?' "

Morrison continued to read. "Can you believe this? They're already referring to the ship as the twenty-first-century *Titanic*."

No one spoke.

"My ship," Morrison added, his voice breaking. "Now, you two get out of here and make sure nothing else happens before we reach port."

Captain Fairfax and John Saunders nodded and left the room. Morrison settled down into a comfortable chair, tapped his phone and looked at the emails from his office. There was one from his chief financial officer ten minutes earlier saying that thirty passengers who were scheduled to board the ship in Southampton had canceled their reservations.

He got up immediately and went to the bar. This time he chose Johnny Walker Blue and filled his glass. As he sipped, his thought was, That was *before* what happened to Brenda Martin. I wonder how much I will have to pay for her sore throat.

83

Ten hours after he fell asleep, Roger Pearson opened his eyes. I'm alive, I'm alive, he thought. He was aware that he was breathing through a ventilator tube and that his forehead felt hot when he touched it. But I think I'm going to be okay.

He glanced to the side and saw that a man in a white doctor's coat was asleep in the reclining chair next to his bed. He realized that was just as well. He wanted to give his name and say that he had gone overboard from *Queen Charlotte*. He had a very clear memory of the maniacal expression on Yvonne's face as she charged at him and with all her strength shoved him backwards. He certainly intended to let her know that he was very aware of what she had done, but he was not ready to share what happened with whoever on this ship was going to ask him questions.

Roger closed his eyes and gave in to his sense of being blissfully warm and tucked into heavy blankets. As long as I live, I'll never go swimming again, he thought, as the memory of being freezing cold, and trying to spit out the salty water, flooded his mind.

84

"Willy, we've got to put our heads together," Alvirah said firmly, even as she grasped his arm to balance herself against the rolling ship.

"Steady, honey, I've got you," Willy said calmly, while holding Alvirah's arm with one hand and the railing with the other.

"Let's go into one of the quiet rooms," Alvirah suggested. "We need to talk."

"I thought you wanted to walk."

"No, I don't. You never know if someone might be able to hear us."

"I think we're the only ones out here, but okay."

They settled in the English Tea Room and ordered cups of coffee. When she was sure that the waiter was back in the kitchen with the door closed, Alvirah whispered, "Willy, we have to figure all this out now."

Willy took a deep, satisfying sip. "Honey, I'm more worried about what to do with this darn necklace than I am about anything else."

"Don't worry. We'll figure that out," Alvirah said confidently. "But let's consider what we know so far. Somebody killed poor Lady Em and tried to rob her. We know her killer didn't get the Cleopatra necklace because she had given it to Celia. And we know that just before she died, Lady Em told Celia that Roger Pearson, God rest him, and Brenda Martin were cheating her."

Willy nodded. "I believe every word of what Celia said, don't you?"

"Of course. If Celia was guilty, why would she have given us the necklace?" Alvirah paused. "But that isn't the point."

"Then what is?"

"Oh Willy, it's as plain as the nose on your face. Whoever killed Lady Em was going after the necklace. And when he or she didn't get it, the killer decided that Brenda had it and went after her."

"He or she?" Willy asked.

"Of course, it could be either one. And you know who my bet is?" It was a rhetorical question. "I put my money on Yvonne."

"Yvonne?"

"Willy, let's put aside for the moment this Man with One Thousand Faces. Nobody's even sure if he's on the ship. Let's focus on Yvonne. Look at the way she's been all over the ship since her husband fell — or was pushed — over."

Willy's brow creased. "You mean you think Yvonne pushed Roger overboard?"

"I don't say I believe it, but it's entirely possible. I mean, look at her. She didn't miss a breakfast. She's been hanging around with her two Hamptons friends. I've been keeping an eye on them, and I'll tell you this, Yvonne is no brokenhearted widow. I mean, how would you feel if I fell overboard?"

"It never would have happened," Willy said firmly. "First of all, I wouldn't have let you sit on the railing. And second, I would have grabbed you as you started to fall. And if I couldn't stop you from falling, I'd have gone over too so I could help you."

Alvirah's eyes softened. "I know you would, and that's why I love you so much," she said. "But I have to say that Yvonne isn't the only one I have my eye on. Who else? Anna DeMille —"

Willy interrupted. "The one who tells the stupid joke about not being related to Cecil B. DeMille?"

"Exactly. I think she's harmless."

"I agree," Willy said as he finished his coffee. "She's too busy try-ing to land Devon Michaelson to get involved with killing some-body for a necklace."

"Agreed. Scratch her off the list. Now let's talk about the other people at our two tables. There's Professor Longworth."

"The Shakespeare scholar." Willy shook his head. "I don't know about him. He strikes me as a little odd, but not the killer type. But what about Ted Cavanaugh? He was certainly trying to cozy up to Lady Em."

"Yes, he was," Alvirah agreed. "But somehow I can't picture him killing Lady Em. And why would he do it? Celia said that Lady Em was planning to give the Cleopatra necklace to the museum in Cairo."

"That's what Cavanaugh wanted, but did he know that at the time Lady Em was killed?"

Alvirah shook her head dismissively. "Celia probably didn't tell him, because it would have meant admitting that she saw Lady Em the night before she died. I'm pretty sure we're the only ones Celia trusted with that information. But I just don't believe Cavanaugh would kill anyone. He's from such a nice family. I mean his father was an ambassador twice."

"A lot of people from nice families turn out to be killers," Willy commented.

Alvirah ignored that possibility. "Let's think about it. Who else has been at our tables?"

"Devon Michaelson?"

"Oh, of course, he could be the one, but somehow I don't think so. I mean, he was on this ship to scatter his wife's ashes, poor soul. He probably spends most of his time hiding from Anna DeMille. Let's get back to Professor Longworth. He travels a lot. He's a regular speaker on these cruises, just as Celia is."

"Except that Longworth is retired. Celia has a full-time job at Carruthers."

"She *hopes* she has a full-time job. She doesn't know what's going to happen because that miserable former fiancé of hers has been trying to portray her as a thief."

"Well, he'll have no luck, I'm sure of that."

"He may have no luck tying her to his fraud, but that hasn't stopped him from making Celia's life miserable."

"And honey, I'm getting worried. What are we going to do with this necklace when we get to Southampton or when we fly home?" As he spoke, Willy fumbled in his pants pocket but then was reassured when his fingers touched the emerald necklace.

"We get home, call Ted Cavanaugh and turn the necklace over to him."

"And how do we explain that we have it?"

"I'm still working on that," Alvirah said. "Giving the necklace to Ted is what Lady Em wanted. Ted is right. It belongs to the people of Egypt. Cleopatra was their queen."

"A lot of luck it brought her." Willy stared at his empty cup but knew Alvirah would not want him to signal the waiter back.

"I still have questions about Yvonne," Alvirah reflected, "but think about it this way: someone will do anything, even kill, to get that necklace, agreed?"

"Agreed," Willy echoed.

"That someone killed Lady Em and tried to kill Brenda, but still didn't get the necklace."

"That makes sense, at least as far as we can figure it so far."

"The Captain could have announced that the necklace was secure in his safe, but he hasn't done that. What does that tell the killer?"

"That somebody else, one of the passengers, has it."

"So if you're the killer, whether you're somebody we know on the ship or this Man with One Thousand Faces, and you're trying to figure out who has the necklace, and you know it wasn't Lady Em or Roger or Brenda, who would you guess has it?"

"Celia Kilbride," Willy said promptly.

"That's the way my mind is going," Alvirah confirmed. "There's no question that with the killer still on the loose, Celia is in grave danger."

She looked down and realized she had only swallowed a few sips of her coffee. Resisting the urge to grab it, she pushed it over to Willy. "I've been watching you staring at your empty cup. You could use a little more."

"Thank you," Willy said, as he eagerly reached for the cup.

"Willy, it's up to you and me to make sure that nothing happens to Celia before we get to Southampton."

"*If* we get to Southampton," Willy said, as they felt a particularly dramatic roll of the ship.

Day Six

85

After speaking to Alvirah and Ted, Celia reveled in the luxurious feeling of having nothing to do. No more lectures, she thought, just a final day of R & R before Southampton.

She threw back the down comforter, got out of bed, stretched and walked over to her balcony door. She slid it back and felt a stiff, cool, breeze, which made her nightgown flutter. The sea that had been very stormy and rough yesterday was only slightly calmer this morning.

Celia phoned and ordered scrambled eggs, an English muffin and coffee. When it was delivered, there was the daily newspaper also on the tray. She was tempted to ignore it, but she couldn't resist the temptation to glance through it.

Not surprisingly, there was no mention of what happened to Lady Em or the necklace, but there was a notice about Steven's case. His bail had been raised after the *People* magazine article in which he openly admitted guilt, the judge saying that he considered Steven an enhanced flight risk. "You bet he is," Celia said aloud. She pushed away the thought that as soon as she got home she would have to meet with the FBI to be questioned again.

She finished breakfast, lingered over coffee, then slowly got up and turned on both the shower and the steamer in her bathroom. This is heaven, she thought, as she stood in the shower and washed her hair. She felt as though every pore in her body was expelling fear and apprehension. She turned off the shower, put lotion on her face and body and felt infinitely refreshed.

As she dressed, her mind was elsewhere. She was trying to work out what she would say if it became known that she had had the Cleopatra necklace in her suite the night of Lady Em's murder.

Why would anyone believe that Lady Em *gave* it to me? she wondered. The answer was, they wouldn't. Focus on the present, she ordered herself as she tied her robe back on, turned on the hair dryer and brushed her hair. After touching up her face with makeup, she went to the closet. She pulled out the new workout suit she had bought for the trip.

Don't be silly, she told herself as she dressed. Ted Cavanaugh doesn't have the slightest interest in me, especially after that article in *People*. He's the kind of guy any woman would want. He was just being thoughtful when he asked me to have lunch with him.

It was still early, but when she was finished dressing, she looked in the mirror. She then went to the safe and took out the small gold earrings that her father had given her when she left for college.

He had said, "They were your mother's. Now I want you to have them." Then he added, "You have her face, her eyes and her laugh."

What was my mother like? Celia asked herself. I suppose I should have missed her more than I did, but I was so young and Daddy was always there for me, day and night. I wonder if I demanded too much from him. Maybe he would have met and fallen in love with someone else if he hadn't always been so concerned about me. It wasn't a pleasant thought. I've been so selfish to blame him for my problems. It would have been more honest to blame myself. I've been blaming him for dying before I met Steven, for not being there to give advice.

What made me so anxious to fall in love? I was stupid. Absolutely stupid. But I know one thing. Daddy is with my mother, and I'm sure that he is happy.

She did not have time to pursue that thought, as the phone rang. It was Ted. "Is it okay if I come by in a few minutes to pick you up?"

"All set whenever you are."

When he tapped on the door, she opened it. She could see the approval in his eyes as he linked her hand in his. "It's pretty rocky out there," he said. "I think it would be a good idea to hold on to each other."

Celia snapped her lips closed before she could say, "Gladly, Ted, gladly."

86

Gregory Morrison went to the Queen's Lounge for breakfast reluctantly. He had no desire to see the questioning looks on people's faces or answer their stupid questions about whether he thought anyone else was going to be suffocated or strangled. But it would look as if he were hiding from them if he took his meals in his room.

As if he didn't have enough to worry about, Captain Fairfax had called him to say the storm was intensifying instead of diminishing. Dr. Blake told him the infirmary was getting overwhelmed by passengers with cases of seasickness. This is just great, he thought to himself bitterly. On my beautiful ship, if you were lucky enough to not get suffocated or strangled, you spent part of the voyage with your head in the toilet.

He had one consolation. Brenda Martin had not already come to her table. She's probably in the galley torturing the pastry chef, he decided.

The truth was that the rolling of the ship had made Brenda queasy. She had been forced to cancel her plan to make her way to the lower three floors and regale the rest of the passengers by sharing her damsel-in-distress story with them.

Professor Longworth and Yvonne were at the table. Morrison was too distracted to realize that Yvonne was eyeing him with interest. She had researched him online and learned that he had been divorced for ten years and had no children. Besides being the sole owner of *Queen Charlotte*, he was also the owner of a fleet of twenty ships that specialized in river cruises. He's sixty-six, she thought. About twenty years older than me, but that's not too bad. I'll have to invite him to visit East Hampton around Easter.

She smiled as Morrison chose a seat next to her. What was he saying? Oh, yes, "Did you realize that *Queen Charlotte* is in no way responsible when a passenger falls overboard?" We'll see about that, she thought, as she gave him an even bigger smile. Then she noticed that a crew member had rushed over to Captain Fairfax and was whispering something to him. She watched as a surprised expression came over the Captain's face, and he hurried over to Morrison.

"I need to have a word with you, Mr. Morrison. Please excuse us, ma'am," Fairfax said as they moved a few feet away. The Captain spoke too softly for her to hear, but there was no mistaking Morrison's response: "You mean the poor guy was floating for almost eleven hours?"

Oh, no, oh my God, no, Yvonne thought, but she made sure her expression revealed none of that as Morrison walked quickly toward her and said, "Wonderful news, Mrs. Pearson. Your husband was picked up by a passing ship. He has pneumonia, but he is recovering fast. He'll be in Southampton one day after us."

"Oh, I don't know what to say," Yvonne managed to utter before she closed her eyes and fainted.

87

Time was running out. Tomorrow at dawn they would dock in Southampton. There was less than twenty-four hours left to get the Cleopatra necklace. He had been so sure that Brenda was the one Lady Em would have trusted with it. Obviously, he had been wrong.

Who else? he asked himself as he paced the promenade deck.

It did not trouble him in the least that Brenda had lived. Her account about what happened in her room made it clear she had no idea who attacked her. He wondered what had motivated her to make up a story that her assailant had stolen a pearl necklace from her room.

By pulling the pillowcase over her head and then throwing her in the closet, he had been able to search her cabin. The Cleopatra necklace was not there.

He had not wanted to kill Brenda any more than he had wanted to kill Lady Em. But Lady Em woke up in time to get a clear look at him and might have seen through his disguise. With Brenda, it was a close call. He hadn't even closed the door to his room when he heard the butler knocking on the door to her suite.

At the Captain's cocktail party he had overheard the Captain asking Lady Em to allow him to keep the necklace in his private safe. Suppose she had changed her mind and decided to give it to him?

She had not been feeling well that last night. But she had the necklace on as she went back to her room.

She had refused to let Brenda accompany her. Actually, Lady Em had appeared very cool toward Brenda that evening. He wondered if she was mad at her for some reason. If so, this would explain why she didn't call Brenda to come and take the necklace.

Who was left that she might have trusted? Probably Roger, but he had fallen overboard. She didn't seem close to Yvonne. And certainly Yvonne looked bored whenever Lady Em spoke. The Man with One Thousand Faces was angry at himself. He should have thought this through more carefully before he went to Brenda's room and waited for her.

Was there anyone else? His mind kept returning to Celia Kilbride. Lady Em had made it a point to have the young gemologist sit at her table. She had been in the front row for both of her jewelry lectures. It was apparent from one of the questions Lady Em asked that the two knew each other and had a cordial relationship. Lady Em appeared to enjoy talking to Celia more than she did to her late financial advisor or her personal assistant.

Did the Captain's request to put the necklace in his safe make her nervous? Had he told her that the Man with One Thousand Faces might be on board? If that had happened and all of a sudden she was worried about the necklace, whom would she trust with it? It made sense. She would give it to the friendly young gemologist.

He reached into his sports jacket and searched the passenger registry for Celia Kilbride's name. Her room was a short walk down the hallway from Lady Em's suite.

She has to be the one, he decided.

88

Yvonne was helped to her cabin by two stewards. She asked them
to settle her into one of the club chairs and then insisted they leave.
The ramifications of Roger having survived the fall were settling in
on her. What do I do if he says I pushed him? she asked herself. I
will absolutely deny it. We both had had a lot to drink. I already said
I was in the restroom before he went over. Then when I came out
and he wasn't there, I was so afraid that something might have happened. That's when I called for help.

That sounds good and reasonable, she assured herself. She then
realized she had another card to play. Nobody knows who killed
Lady Em. I'll tell Roger that I did it to protect him from going to
prison. I don't think Lady Em told anyone else about the planned
audit.

I'll make it all right. I know I can. And if he doesn't believe
me, I'll tell him I'll go straight to the police and tell them about
Lady Em's problem with her finances. That will do the trick.

Valerie and Dana must know by now that Roger's alive. What do
I say to them? I'll tell them that when I received word that he was
alive, all I wanted to do was give our marriage another chance. I
knew that in our hearts we could fall in love again.

They'll fall for it. I'm a very good actress.

89

Ted held Celia's hand firmly and with the other hand braced himself against the railing of the corridor. "Why don't we go down to the main deck?" he said. "The theory is that it's the most stable spot on the ship."

"Sounds good to me," Celia agreed.

"I don't think it will be crowded," Ted said. "It's too bad our last full day at sea is like this."

They were the only ones on the elevator. When they got off on the main deck, the ship was discernibly calmer. The Tap Room was small, with a private bar. When they sat down, Ted opened the menu for her. "What's your choice? After a glass of Chardonnay, of course," he added with a smile.

"I've had so much rich food. Does grilled cheese, tomato and bacon on rye toast sound pedestrian?"

"Yes, it does," Ted said. "Let's order two."

When the waitress came, he gave their order, and then when she was gone, he looked across the table at Celia. "I know you said you slept well. Does that mean you're feeling better about things?"

"Yes, I am," Celia said frankly. "And let me tell you why. I know I told you yesterday how much I missed my father, but then I realized I was angry with him for dying and for not remarrying so I would have brothers and sisters. Over several cups of coffee this morning, I realized what a nerve I had to blame him. And I realized how very selfish I had been. He was there for me 24/7 all my life. Who knows if he had taken more time for himself, if he would have met someone?"

"That's a pretty big leap," Ted observed.

"A necessary one," Celia said. "And now I've told you all about myself, maybe more than you wanted to hear."

"I hope you know I was very flattered that you took me into your confidence," Ted said.

"I appreciate that," Celia responded. "But now it's your turn. Tell me about yourself and your family."

Ted leaned back. "Well, let's see. I think you've heard that my father was ambassador to Egypt—"

"And the Court of St. James's," Celia said.

"Exactly right. My parents were married right after they graduated from Princeton. My father went on to law school, and eventually became a federal judge. My mother would have happily lived in Westchester County all her life and raised us there, but my father was offered a job as a diplomatic attaché in Egypt. We moved there when I was six years old. My two little brothers were born there."

"Where did you go to school?" Celia asked.

"I went to the American International School in Cairo. That's where most of the diplomats' kids went. I was there for eight years, and then my father was made ambassador to the Court of St. James's. So we were in London the four years he served there."

"I think I detect a slight British accent. Am I right?"

"You are right," Ted said. "I was at Eton for my high school years. Then I went to Princeton and on to Yale Law School."

"Did you enjoy living abroad?"

"I enjoyed it very much. Along the way I became fascinated by how British and Egyptian culture interacted over the years."

"Do you miss living abroad?"

"No, to be perfectly honest, I don't. I loved every minute of it, and I'm happy to travel back. One of my clients is Egypt's minister of state for antiquities. I work to recover lost and stolen Egyptian artifacts throughout Europe and the United States. But like my mother, my preference is to live in the New York area."

"That's really interesting. How did you end up in the area of law you're practicing?"

"Like so many things in life, it was chance. In my third year of law school I wasn't sure what I wanted to do. I was interviewing with several of the big name litigation firms in New York. I saw a notice for this small, quirky Manhattan law firm that specialized in recovering stolen antiquities. Part of the job description said, 'Familiarity with Egypt a plus.'

"Of course, I was intrigued. I went on the interview. There were two older partners looking to bring in new blood. We hit it off. I went with them. After being there seven years, they made me a partner."

"Where in the city are you?"

"Our office is on Sixth Avenue and Forty-Seventh Street. I have an apartment in Greenwich Village, three subway stops away."

"By yourself?" Celia asked.

"Definitely," he said emphatically. "And may I assume your living status is the same?"

"Absolutely, definitely," Celia confirmed.

They had finished the sandwiches. "I think this calls for a second glass of wine," Ted suggested.

"At the risk of repeating myself, absolutely, definitely," she agreed.

All morning Celia had wondered if she could confide in Ted about her last conversation with Lady Em. She waited until the waiter had delivered their wines and left.

"I want your opinion as a lawyer on what I'm about to tell you," she said as she took a sip of the cold Chardonnay.

"I'll be happy to give it to you, and I promise our conversation will be confidential," Ted said, his eyes narrowing as he listened.

"On the night Lady Em died, I had just gotten back to my room around ten o'clock. Lady Em phoned and asked me to come to her suite right away and to bring my loupe. When I got there, she was not feeling well and was visibly upset. She told me she was sure that both her financial advisor, Roger Pearson—"

"The one who went overboard?"

"Yes, and her personal assistant, Brenda, were cheating her. She handed me a bracelet and asked me to look at it. It was clearly a piece of junk. My examination confirmed that it was not the very expensive bracelet her husband had given her many years ago. She said she had no idea how many of her other pieces Brenda might have stolen and substituted over the years. Then she told me that earlier that morning she had told Roger that she was planning to have an outside accountant go over her financial affairs. She said she was very afraid that their conversation might have played a role in his going overboard that evening."

Celia looked at Ted and could not gauge his response. "Lastly, and of great importance to you, Lady Em handed me the Cleopatra necklace. She asked me to take it to my room and give it to the Captain in the morning. She told me that she had changed her mind, she agreed with you, it belonged to the people of Egypt. She planned to turn it over to you when she got back to New York."

"I had no idea," Ted said.

"She did not want to put you in a position of suing the Smithsonian for it and having her husband and father-in-law's names dragged into a scandal. Her understanding was that her father-in-law had paid a great deal of money for the necklace."

"Where is it now?" Ted asked.

Celia took a deep breath and then continued. "You know about my problem with my former fiancé and his fund. When I learned that Lady Em had been murdered during the night, I realized I was in a terrible predicament."

"I can understand that," Ted said soothingly. "If I can ask again, where is the necklace?"

"I had to figure out who I could trust. I turned to Alvirah Meehan and explained the predicament I was in. She suggested I give the necklace to her and that Willy would hold on to it."

"Celia, you did a really smart thing to protect the necklace. No one will suspect that Willy Meehan has it. But now I'm very worried about *you*. Whoever suffocated Lady Em and tried to kill Brenda clearly was looking for the necklace. Anybody who was watching Lady Em since this cruise began could easily see that you and she had become very friendly. Lady Em's financial advisor didn't have the necklace and Brenda didn't have the necklace. Who does that leave?" He gently pointed at her. "You."

Celia exhaled. "I was so worried about the necklace. I never really thought about that."

"Celia, you've been through an awfully rough patch. Given a little time, the situation with your former boyfriend will sort itself out, and you will be fine. But right now, it's time to be very careful. Whoever is after that necklace knows that tonight is his last chance. You cannot go into or out of your suite alone. You must always double lock your door. In addition to being your new attorney, I have elected myself your escort."

"Thank you, Counselor, that is a very big relief."

Ted's hand reached across the table and took hers. "In my work I have dealt with some very unsavory characters and lived to tell the tale. Nothing is going to happen to you while I'm around," he promised.

90

Morrison was delighted to see that Celia Kilbride had joined the table. Her presence made it much easier for him to spend time there. *And I will say she's a beautiful woman*, he thought, as he walked across the room.

To his dismay he realized the dining room was half-empty. The final meal was supposed to be festive. It was a time when contact information was exchanged to cement new friendships.

He consoled himself with the good news he had received from his sales office that morning. Even though publicity that followed Lady Em's murder and the attack on Brenda had generated cancelations, new passengers had been calling the reservations office to snap up the now-available rooms. He was not happy to hear that vendors were waiting at the Southampton dock to sell I SURVIVED MY QUEEN CHARLOTTE CRUISE T-shirts.

I'll be glad to see the last of this group, he thought, as he nodded to the next table and then smiled broadly at Celia and Professor Longworth.

Then to his annoyance, he realized that Brenda had arrived and had made no effort to cover the raw marks on her throat. Miracle of miracles, she's recovered her appetite, he thought. I wonder how many new people she managed to talk to before she came to dinner.

There was one thing he was sure of: she wouldn't be sailing on *Queen Charlotte* again. His office had confirmed that Lady Em had paid for both her, the almost-merry widow Yvonne and her now-rescued husband.

Glancing around, he was glad to see that Fairfax was at the Captain's table entertaining a new group of passengers.

He knew that as a courtesy he should ask Yvonne if she had been able to contact her waterlogged husband. He noticed that instead of the gray she had been wearing, in anticipation he was sure, of changing into black, this time she had on a rose-colored jacket and matching slacks. She confirmed that she had spoken to the doctor on the ship. Roger was recovering nicely but had been asleep when she called. She told them not to wake him up and left a loving message for him.

It almost brings a tear to my eye, Morrison thought, with a sneer.

He turned to Celia. He liked the navy-blue jacket she was wearing and the simple scarf tucked around her neck. "Despite the sadness of Lady Em's passing," he began, "I hope you had some pleasure on this trip, Ms. Kilbride."

"It was a privilege to be on this beautiful ship," she said sincerely.

Feeling left out, Brenda blurted, "Mr. Morrison, I do hope we will be able to quickly and amicably settle our differences after my," she paused, "room invasion. But after that's over, I know my close friend and I will welcome the opportunity to sail with you again. As your guests, of course," she added directly.

Morrison tried to bare his teeth in a smile. The first course had been served, and he noticed that Brenda had plowed her way through a generous serving of caviar and signaled for more.

Professor Longworth knew it was time to make his presence

known. "I can only say what a delight the trip has been," he began, as he heaped caviar onto his plate, "and how much I enjoy being a lecturer on your ships, Mr. Morrison. As the Bard said, 'Parting is such sweet sorrow.'"

My father used to say, "Good riddance," Morrison thought to himself.

91

Ted and Celia had both gone back to their cabins to pack. Their luggage had to be outside their rooms by ten o'clock that evening. Ted had waited until he heard the metallic sound of her double lock being turned before he went to his room.

At 7 P.M. he escorted Celia to the dining room, but she turned down his suggestion that she join his table. "Oh Ted, you know how they discourage table hopping on these cruises. If I want to keep lecturing, I have to follow the rules. And besides, we'll barely be six feet apart."

Reluctantly Ted agreed, but as he sat down he realized he was viewing his fellow passengers at both tables as if with a different set of eyes. He glanced warmly at Alvirah and Willy, knowing that Celia trusted them. He knew now that Willy had the Cleopatra necklace, probably in his pocket, and it was surely safe with him. Willy was a big, strong man, with well-muscled forearms. Anyone who tried to steal something from him would have quite a fight on his hands.

He eliminated Anna DeMille from consideration. She certainly looked the part of someone who was going on her first cruise. She had won a church raffle. It was her first trip abroad. If the Man with One Thousand Faces was a woman, she was the last person on the ship he would suspect.

Devon Michaelson? Unlikely, he thought. I believe his story

about being here to scatter his wife's ashes. And the way he's trying to resist Anna's overtures is consistent with a grieving widower.

Having satisfied himself with his tablemates, he glanced at the next table. He knew immediately that he did not like Gregory Morrison. He may own the ship, he thought, but it must have cost a fortune to build. Lady Em's necklace would be a big prize for him to get. Of course, nobody could risk trying to sell it. But every one of those three-strand emeralds would bring him a fortune on the jewelry market.

As he thought about it more, Ted wondered if for Morrison, having the Cleopatra necklace, just like having this ship, would be one more larger-than-life trophy. Even hidden from view, to Morrison the necklace would be an affirmation of his success in the world. He could indeed have anything he wanted, and would do anything to get it.

Morrison could definitely be a suspect. Also, Ted did not like the way the ship owner moved his chair nearer to Celia's.

What about Yvonne? If Lady Em had threatened an outside review of Roger Pearson's handling of her affairs, it was quite possible that she too would have been found complicit in his bilking of the estate.

She's not brilliant, Ted decided, but she is smart enough and maybe vicious enough to protect herself any way she can.

Brenda Martin? No. She couldn't have choked herself, and what would have been the point? Celia already had the Cleopatra necklace.

Professor Longworth? Of course, a possibility, but not much of a probability. Ted knew that he traveled widely, giving lectures at top universities as well as on cruise ships all over the world. Including Egypt. But he was definitely someone to keep in mind.

Ted's eyes shifted to the Captain's table. What about Fairfax? He moved easily all over the world, and he had been the one to urge Lady Em to turn the necklace over to him. Was he upset when she turned him down? Upset enough to kill her? On the other hand, if she had given it to him, he would have had no good way to refuse to give it back to her or her estate. So he wasn't much of a bet to be the murderer and thief.

Dissatisfied with his own reckoning, Ted turned his attention back to the table. He noticed that, as usual, Anna DeMille was brushing her arm against Michaelson. Dear God, but she is a pest, Ted thought. Poor Michaelson. If Anna DeMille goes overboard, he will be on the short list of suspects.

In an attempt to contribute to the conversation Ted asked, " I am sure everyone is packed by now?"

"We are," Alvirah announced.

"So am I," Anna volunteered. "Although I have to say I had tears in my eyes when I closed the suitcase and thought that I may never see any of you again." Her comment was clearly addressed to Devon Michaelson, who flushed an angry red.

Alvirah tried to break the tension. "We'd love to keep in touch with you, Anna." Ignoring Willy's look of dismay, she pulled out a sheet of paper from her purse and scribbled their email address on it. For a moment she hesitated, then decided to skip putting their home address and phone number. Willy is at the end of his patience with me, she thought.

The final evening meal was exquisite. They all agreed on that. Once again it was a caviar appetizer; fillet of sole or roast beef; a salad; cheesecake and ice cream with mixed berries in a liquor sauce; coffee, espresso, cappuccino or tea.

The wine flowed with each course. Ted found himself remembering fondly the grilled cheese, bacon and tomato sandwich at lunch. I don't want any more gourmet food for at least a year, he thought.

Willy's comment was along the same lines. "Back to the gym the minute we reach New York," he said firmly.

"Me too," Alvirah sighed. "I doubt if I'll fit back into my fancy clothes for a while. And I was doing so good on my diet."

Anna DeMille sighed. "I don't get food anything like this in Kansas." She glanced lovingly at Devon. "How's the food in Montreal?"

Devon appeared increasingly frustrated that once again he was being put in a position of either appearing to be rude or having to participate in a conversation he had no interest in.

"Montreal is a very cosmopolitan city. You can find almost any type of food there."

"I'm sure you can. I've always wanted to visit there. When I looked on my computer this morning, I was pleasantly surprised to see that there are direct flights from Kansas City to Montreal."

At the next table the dinner was drawing to a close. Morrison had no intention of staying all evening, but he was becoming increasingly intrigued by Celia. He had figured out who she looked like. Jackie Kennedy, of course. One of the most beautiful and intelligent women who had ever set foot in the White House.

As they finished coffee, he said, "Celia, I go back and forth to my office in New York. As you can understand, I can't stay on the ship for the entire three-month around-the-world sail. I do hope that I may have the pleasure of having you dine with me very soon in Manhattan or having you join me for vacations on my ship."

Ted had overheard and in an instant was standing behind Celia's chair. For the benefit of Morrison and all others within hearing distance, he asked, "Ready to go, dear?"

Her smile answered his question. As if a silent signal had been passed, everyone stood up and said good night. Since it was going to be a very early morning, there was no suggestion of having a final nightcap.

92

"That guy was trying to hit on you," Ted said, his mouth in an angry, tight line.

"He sure was," Willy chimed in as he pushed the button for the elevator. "Just because he owns this ship, what makes him think he has any right to start rubbing your arm?"

"He's a disgrace," Alvirah said firmly, but her mind was elsewhere.

As they started down the corridor to their rooms, she turned to Celia. "I have to say that I am very nervous about your being alone," she began. "As we all know, someone managed to get into Lady Em's room and Brenda's room as well. And I bet my bottom dollar that whoever is looking for the Cleopatra necklace has figured out that Lady Em gave it to you."

"I absolutely agree," Ted said emphatically. "Now, what do we do about it?"

"I put my thinking cap on, and I have a great idea," Alvirah volunteered. "Celia, you should come in with me, and Willy can sleep in your room. I can tell you this right now. Nobody is going to suffocate or strangle Willy."

"I think that's an excellent idea," Ted agreed.

Celia shook her head. "No way. We're all stressed out. I'm not going to have Willy lying awake most of the night and Alvirah worrying about him. I promise I'll put the chain on my door. No one's going to get in with it on."

It was apparent to Alvirah, Willy and Ted that there would be no persuading Celia to change her mind. Alvirah and Willy were three doors down from Ted. Celia was three more down from Ted and across the hall. When Willy and Alvirah said good night, Ted walked Celia to her room.

"Celia, I'm so worried about you," he said. "Would you let me curl up on the big chair in your sitting room?"

Celia shook her head. "Thank you, but no."

"I thought that would be your answer," Ted said. "But I insist on going in and making sure your room is safe. When you lock that door, I want to be one hundred percent certain that you are the only one inside."

Celia nodded as she inserted the electronic key in the lock. Ted went in ahead of her. "Wait here, please," he said as he walked quickly across the room and pulled open the closet doors. She watched as he entered the bedroom area, opened the doors of the armoire and got down on one knee and looked under the bed. He then slid open the glass door to the balcony, went outside and looked around.

"I'm glad I left the suite neat or this could have been really embarrassing," Celia said.

"Celia, please. This is no time for jokes. I want to ask you one last time—"

Celia shook her head. "I really appreciate the offer, but no. We all have to get up early and then we'll be herded off the ship. I promise if someone tries to come into my room, I'll scream like a banshee."

"That doesn't make me feel any better," Ted said. "In Irish folklore a banshee is a spirit in the form of a woman who appears to a family and wails when someone is about to die."

"I thought I was the expert on legends," Celia said with a smile. "I'll be fine, Counselor."

"You're very stubborn," Ted said as he put his arms around her. To his dismay he realized how thin and fragile she seemed. He was sure that the stress of her ex-fiancé's arrest and the accusations against her had caused her to lose weight.

"Okay. You win," Ted said. "I want to hear you double lock the door."

"Right now, immediately," Celia promised. With a quick kiss on her forehead, Ted pulled the door closed behind him and stood there until he heard the faint rattle of the chain sliding into place.

For a moment he stayed outside the door as every instinct told him not to leave. But then, with a sigh, he turned, went down the corridor to his room and stepped inside.

93

In his usual way Willy fell into a deep sleep the minute he shed his clothes and got into bed. His T-shirt and boxers were always his chosen night garments, despite Alvirah's gifts of pajamas and robes. These gifts were promptly exchanged for shirts and chinos.

Alvirah's nightwear was a comfortable long-sleeved nightgown. A cotton robe was always placed at the foot of the bed. Her glasses were always in one of the pockets as well as a bottle of Tylenol in case her increasing arthritis threatened her rest.

Like Willy, she fell asleep quickly. Unlike him, she awoke a few hours later. With a start, she realized that her usual secure and comfortable position, her shoulder wedged over Willy's, was not working.

She was on edge, troubled, deeply worried about Celia. Why wouldn't she come in here and stay with me? she fretted. Suppose someone got into her room? Brenda is a big strong woman, but she had been overpowered by whoever broke into her room. What chance would Celia have in a struggle?

And so it went. The first soft whistle of Willy's snore, usually a source of comfort, did little to reassure her.

94

It was now or never. The Man with One Thousand Faces deliberately walked up the two flights of stairs to avoid meeting anyone in the corridor. He stepped slowly into his suite and began to put his plan into action.

The first order of business was to completely change his appearance. Although he was almost certain that no one had seen him the nights he had broken into Lady Em's and Brenda's rooms, he would use a different disguise. It began with his eyes. Taking dark brown contact lenses out of a box, he slipped them in. That's the easy part, he thought; the next part takes time and skill. He opened his makeup kit, glanced in the mirror and began practicing an art that had started when he volunteered to work on theatrical productions during his high school days.

A face cream turned his complexion sallow. Eyebrow pencil turned his thin brows into a dark, belligerent midnight-brown. Slashes of deep lines totally altered his face. He pasted into place a medium-length graying beard. Satisfied that it was on straight, he took a brown wig, stretched it over his head and patted it into place. Experience had taught him that a potential witness would be more likely to focus on the contrast between the dark hair and the graying beard, and spend less time looking at the face.

He took a long slow look at himself in the mirror, turning his head from side to side. Excellent, he thought with satisfaction. He reached into his suitcase for the shoes. The lifts on them would add three inches to his height.

He pulled on the butler's jacket he had stolen from the kitchen on his floor. It was a reasonably good fit, with some extra room in the shoulders and waist. He took masking tape from a compartment in his suitcase and slipped it in the jacket's side pocket. A pair of wire cutters was carefully placed in the opposite pocket.

For the next fifteen minutes he practiced limping slightly to the left and dragging his foot on the ground.

95

A few hours later Alvirah awakened with a start. She felt her heart racing as she tried to calm herself after dreaming about Celia. There's no way I'm going to fall back to sleep, she thought, as she pulled on her robe and went into the outer room of her suite.

Not quite sure why, she opened the door to the hallway. The soft light made her eyes blink. I should go down to Celia's room, knock on her door and make sure she's okay, she thought. A glance at her watch made her feel foolish. All Celia needs to really scare her to death is my banging on her door at three-thirty in the morning. I should mind my own business and go back to bed.

She was in the process of closing her door when she heard it. A sound of metal snapping came down the hallway from the direction of Celia's room. Were her ears playing tricks on her? A few moments later she heard a muffled scream. It was over almost as fast as it had begun, but she felt sure she knew what it was.

She was about to go wake up Willy when she changed her mind. Ted can get there faster, she thought, as she raced down the hall, and started banging on Ted's door. "Ted, get up. Celia's in trouble."

Ted jumped at the first sound, raced to the door in his pajamas and threw it open. Alvirah was in the hallway looking terrified. "I heard a noise from Celia's room." Ted didn't wait for her to finish her explanation. He sprinted down the hall in the direction of Celia's suite.

Alvirah's first instinct was to follow him. But then she stopped, hurried back into her room, went over to the bed and shook Willy. "Willy, Willy, wake up. Celia needs us. Come on, Willy, get up." As a dazed Willy pulled on the pants he had laid out for the next morning, Alvirah breathlessly explained what she had heard. She then called security and asked them to send help.

In a heavy sleep, Celia had been vaguely aware of a sound coming from the hallway. The metallic click of wire cutters severing the chain lock on her door had integrated itself into a dream she was having about when she was a little girl in a playground with her father. By the time she recognized the sounds of footsteps growing closer, the intruder was already upon her. She managed a brief scream before a strong hand held a cloth over her mouth. Struggling to breathe, she looked up to see a stranger's face hovering over her. In the stranger's other hand a pistol was pointed at her forehead.

"Make another sound and you'll join your friend Lady Em. Do you understand?" Although terrified, Celia nodded her head in agreement. She felt the pressure on the cloth over her mouth ease, only to be replaced by something cool and sticky over her lips and chin. It was some type of tape. Unlike when the cloth had covered her nose, she was now able to breathe freely. She had no idea who her attacker was, but she thought there was something vaguely familiar about his voice.

He started speaking again as he tied her hands in front of her, and then her feet. When he spoke, his voice was surprisingly calm and measured. "Celia, it's up to you, whether or not you die tonight. Give me what I want and your friends will find you here safe in the morning. If you want to live, tell me where the Cleopatra necklace is. And I'm warning you, don't lie to me. I know you have it."

Celia nodded her head. She was desperate to buy time so that— so that what? Nobody even knew she was in trouble. I can't tell him Willy has it. He'll kill him and Alvirah.

She yelped in pain as he pulled off the masking tape. "Okay, Celia, where is the necklace?"

"I don't know. I don't have it. I'm sorry, I don't know."

"That's really too bad, Celia. You know there's an old expression. There's nothing like fear to help the mind focus."

The masking tape was slapped back down over her mouth. Strong arms yanked her out of her bed and dragged her toward the balcony door. Keeping one arm around her waist, he opened the door and pushed her out onto the balcony. It was cold and windy. She began to shiver. He hoisted her up into a sitting position on the railing and leaned her over the dark ocean some sixty feet below. His grip on the rope around her hands was the only thing that prevented her from falling.

"All right, Celia, I'm going to ask you one more time who has the necklace," he said as he ripped the tape from her mouth. "If you still don't know, I'll believe you. But then there won't be any point to my holding on to this rope." He loosened his grip and allowed her to fall a little before pulling her back. Celia felt waves of nausea and terror wash over her.

"So what'll it be, Celia? Who has the necklace?"

"She doesn't have it," Ted shouted as he plunged through the door and raced onto the balcony. "Get her down off that railing now!"

The intruder and Ted glared at each other, less than five feet separating them. One hand held the rope that kept Celia from falling; the other held the pistol which now was pointed at Ted's chest.

"Okay, you want to be a hero, where is the necklace?"

"I don't have it, but I can get it," Ted said.

"You're not going anywhere. Get down on your knees. Put your hands behind your head. NOW!"

Ted complied, never taking his eyes off Celia. Although Celia's feet were tied together, he noticed that she had managed to hook her one foot behind the post beneath her.

"All right, Mr. Cavanaugh, tell me where the necklace is, or the little lady goes for a swim."

"Wait," Alvirah yelled as she opened the door and she and Willy raced onto the balcony. "He doesn't have it. It's in our room," Alvirah said. "Free Celia, and we'll take you to it."

As Alvirah was speaking, Willy's hand reached into his pants pocket. He felt the Cleopatra necklace he had hidden there the previous evening and slipped it out of his pocket.

"Is this what you're looking for?" Willy shouted, as he dangled it in front of the intruder, whose eyes focused on the treasure. Willy briefly made eye contact with Ted, who nodded. It was a chance they had to take. "You must really want this a lot if you're willing to kill people for it. Here, take it."

Willy flipped the necklace high in the air toward the intruder, whose only chance to save it from going over the side of the ship was to use his hand that held the pistol. As he reached for it, he released his grip on the rope that held Celia atop the railing. She started to go over backwards, her foot hooking the post, momentarily slowing her fall.

Ted, Alvirah and Willy sprang into action. Ted leapt up, reached over the railing and grabbed Celia's arms. The momentum of her fall started to drag him over the railing. Alvirah grabbed hold of Ted's legs and held on for dear life.

Willy had moved immediately when the intruder's attention was on catching the necklace. In the time it took for Willy to move across the balcony, the thief had caught the necklace and was bringing his arm with the pistol back in Willy's direction. With a mighty swipe, Willy smacked the intruder's hand. The pistol fired, narrowly missing Willy's head. The pistol and the necklace clattered to the balcony floor. Willy grabbed the intruder's arms.

Ted was straining every muscle in his body to hold on to Celia. His waist was on the balcony railing as he had broken the momentum of her fall. He had stopped her from falling, but didn't have the strength to pull her back to the height of the railing. A moment later he felt Alvirah's strong grip on his legs, holding him from toppling over.

"Ted, let go," Celia screamed. "You'll fall. You'll fall." Desperately she tried to free her hands from his grip.

Willy and the intruder were glaring at each other. Without his pistol, the intruder was no match for the burly ex-plumber. When Willy glanced at Alvirah and Ted struggling to save Celia, he released his hold on the intruder, who ran off the balcony and through the door.

Ted could feel his upper body slipping farther over the rail. Willy rushed to the railing, reached his long arms over and grabbed Ted's elbows. "Pull her and I'll pull you," he said. With a final desperate effort he was able to pull Ted back toward the balcony. A moment later he and Ted hoisted Celia over the rail. The three of them fell along with Alvirah onto the floor of the balcony, exhausted and gasping for breath.

The intruder knew he needed to make it the short distance back to his room and he would be safe. He was confident that no one would be able to identify him. The wig, beard and jacket he had worn would quickly be tossed into the ocean below.

He pulled open the door to the hallway and froze. Chief of Security John Saunders was holding a pistol that was aimed at his forehead. He dragged him out into the hallway, where Captain Fairfax and Gregory Morrison, both in *Queen Charlotte* bathrobes, held his arms behind his back as Saunders snapped a pair of handcuffs around his wrists and pushed him back into the room.

Ted, his arm around Celia, and Willy, his arm around Alvirah, were staggering into the room.

"Is anyone hurt?" Saunders asked.

It was Ted who answered. "No, I think we're all okay."

"I'm sorry it took us a few extra minutes to get here," Saunders said. Turning to Alvirah he added, "When you phoned security, we mistakenly believed the robbery was taking place in your room. We went there first."

"Sorry," Alvirah said. "It's an old habit to give my room number first when I'm calling."

Willy helped Alvirah into a chair and then moved menacingly across the room at the intruder. "I don't take kindly to anyone pointing a gun at my wife," he said, as his hand shot forward.

The intruder braced himself for the expected blow from Willy's huge fist. But Willy's hand stopped short, grabbed hold of the intruder's beard and gave it a hard yank. A yelp of pain followed as the beard was detached from his face.

After throwing the beard to the floor, Willy grabbed a handful of the intruder's hair and pulled. The wig became detached. Everyone in the room stared at the face of the unmasked assailant.

Willy spoke first. "Well, if it isn't the poor widower who came to scatter his wife's ashes. You're damn lucky I don't scatter you over the Atlantic Ocean."

It was Morrison's turn next, his voice dripping with sarcasm. "Why, it's Inspector Clouseau from Interpol. I knew you were useless. My *Queen Charlotte* has a lovely brig. You will be its first guest."

96

For a moment there was dead silence as Morrison, Saunders and Captain Fairfax shoved Devon Michaelson out of the room. Then as Willy closed the door, Alvirah went to the closet and pulled out a *Queen Charlotte* bathrobe. "Celia, you're freezing. Let's wrap you in this."

Celia let her arms be pushed into it, then felt the sash being tied around her waist. She realized that she must still be in some level of shock. The memory of trying to hold on to the railing with her foot as she felt herself going backwards kept replaying in her mind. It was all over, she had thought, before Ted's arms grabbed hers and saved her from falling. She recalled the feeling of the cold wind against her face and arms, and the ominous sense that she was going to die. Trying to shake the memory, she looked from Alvirah to Willy to Ted.

"I can thank the three of you that I'm not in the ocean," she said. "It's only because of you that I'm not trying to swim to Southampton."

"We'd never let that happen," Alvirah said firmly. "And now we all better get back to bed." She and Willy headed for the door.

Ted closed it behind them.

"This time I'm not taking no for an answer. And something else." He put his arms around Celia. "Will you please tell me why you were trying to get your hands out of mine?" he asked.

"Because I didn't want you to fall. I couldn't let you fall. I put all of you in danger and—"

Ted stopped her with a kiss. "We'll finish this conversation later. Now, let's get you into bed. You're still trembling." He guided her into the bedroom, and after she lay down, he tucked the blankets over her.

"I'm pushing the easy chair against the door and sleeping in it until it's time for us to leave. I don't trust them to hold on to that guy until you're off the ship."

Celia realized how glad she was to not be alone. "No objection, Counselor," she murmured as her eyes began to close.

97

Everyone except Willy was downstairs at 7:30 A.M. as the *Queen Charlotte* began to dock in Southampton. As the word spread through the ship that Devon Michaelson, "the grieving widower" as he had become known, was the killer, shock and surprise was the immediate reaction.

At Lady Em's table Yvonne, Brenda and Professor Longworth stared at each other. "I thought it might be you," Brenda blurted out to Longworth.

"I don't think I'd be nearly strong enough to wrestle you into a closet," Longworth shot back, his voice testy.

Yvonne was silent. Now that the true identity of Lady Em's killer had been revealed, Roger would know that she had not suffocated Lady Em to save him. The ship that had rescued him would arrive in Southampton one day behind *Queen Charlotte*. If he tried to tell people that she had shoved him over the rail, she would say that he was traumatized after his ordeal. And if he got nasty, she would tell him that she would blow the whistle on his stealing from Lady Em.

Celia had come over and sat in the chair that had formerly been Devon Michaelson's at the table with Anna DeMille, Ted and Alvirah. Anna was repeating over and over how she had refused the callous advances made on her by Devon Michaelson.

Devon hitting on her? Alvirah thought sympathetically. I'll certainly keep in touch with the poor thing.

A few minutes later Willy arrived looking relieved. "Alvirah and I spoke to Ted before we came down to breakfast. Ted told us that the necklace is evidence in Lady Em's murder and the attack on Brenda and that the necklace had to be turned over to the FBI. Boy, was I glad to hand it over to them."

There was no lingering at the table. The good-byes had been spoken to newly made friends. The room began to empty when the departing passengers, as one, headed onto the main deck.

Their progress was briefly delayed as two Scotland Yard officials halted the exiting passengers. Through the windows they could see two men in FBI jackets, each holding one of Devon Michaelson's arms, which were handcuffed behind his back. His legs were shackled. They were escorting the suspect down the ramp.

As soon as they had passed through customs, Brenda reached for her cell phone. Aware that it was four o'clock in the morning back in New York, she began to tap out a loving text. She signed it *"Forever, your buttercup."*

Ted had hired a car to take him directly to the airport. He upgraded to an SUV and insisted that Alvirah and Willy and Celia ride with him. They were all sleepy, and there was little conversation on the two-hour trip. He had phoned ahead and booked a first-class reservation for Celia on his flight, in the seat next to him.

Alvirah and Willy were on the same flight in the economy section. "I would never spend the money for first class," Alvirah said flatly. "The back of the plane gets there almost as fast as the front!"

"That's news," Willy muttered. He would have loved to stretch out in first class, but he knew it was hopeless to suggest it.

The plane had barely gone wheels up when all four of them fell asleep, Alvirah in the crook of Willy's arm and Celia with her head nestled on Ted's shoulder.

Somehow the thought of going back and facing further questioning from the FBI was not as scary as it had been only a few days ago. Ted had insisted that he reach out to her lawyer and offer his services and those of his investigators. "We are very good at what we do," he had assured her. She knew that in the end everything would really be okay.

Epilogue

Three Months Later

Alvirah and Willy hosted a celebration dinner for Ted and Celia in their apartment on Central Park South. There was a storm outside and the park was covered with drifting snow. The horses and carriages were *clip-clopping* through it, and the familiar tinkle of their bells added a timeless sense of years gone by.

Inside, over cocktails, the four of them recalled their adventurous week on the *Queen Charlotte*. As promised, Anna DeMille had kept in close touch with Alvirah, saying that nothing could be more exciting than the cruise, even including "that thief making advances at me."

"I still can't get over the news about Devon Michaelson," Alvirah said. Shortly after Michaelson's arrest, Interpol had issued a statement: "Not now or at any time in the past did Interpol have an employee by that name on staff. He obviously presented falsified credentials. An investigation is being conducted to determine whether he had inside help at Castle Lines when he made arrangements to be on that voyage."

"Heads will roll if that happened," Willy said.

Celia had felt compelled to tell the FBI about Lady Em's belief that Brenda had been stealing her jewelry. Part of her felt sorry for

Brenda, but at the same time she believed it was wrong to let a thief go unpunished. But then Ralphie's jeweler friend, the accomplice in switching Lady Em's jewelry, had been arrested and charged in a similar scheme. In exchange for leniency he had quickly given up Ralphie, who in turn had told the FBI about Brenda's role in stealing from Lady Em. Brenda had quickly agreed to a plea deal.

Ted's investigators had succeeded in poking holes in Steven's story that Celia had conspired with him from the beginning in the fund fraud. They had been able to prove that he had begun misappropriating money from client accounts two years before he even knew Celia. When the FBI met with her, their only interest in Celia was as a potential witness against Steven.

At the dinner Ted provided an update on a story they all had been following. It had been in the papers that Lady Em's estate was set to undergo a thorough audit. Several former clients of Roger Pearson's firm had come forward and expressed concern about "irregularities" in the work Roger had done for them. The lawyer Roger retained had put out a statement on his behalf. "Mr. Pearson suffered severe memory loss as a result of his horrific experience at sea and may not be in a position to adequately defend his past work." In the picture, by his side, was his loving wife, Yvonne.

"Let's forget about them," Alvirah suggested, as she held up Champagne in a toast. "Celia, I love your engagement ring," she said. "I'm so happy for both of you."

Celia's ring was a beautiful emerald. "It seemed only fitting to choose that stone," Ted said. "It was emeralds, after all, that brought us together." They had picked it out at Carruthers. Celia's former employer had welcomed her back with open arms and had given her a raise.

Celia thought of Lady Em handing her the Cleopatra necklace. After it was turned over to the FBI, the Smithsonian had issued a statement saying that it was satisfied that Egypt historically was the rightful owner, and that the necklace should be returned to Egypt. The FBI had photographed it as evidence for the criminal trial of Devon Michaelson, and now it was on its way home.

On Christmas Eve they were flying to Sea Island to spend the holiday week with Ted's parents and siblings. Celia thought of how she had felt that first day on the ship, *all by myself, alone.*

As she and Ted exchanged smiles, she thought, all by myself, alone. Never ever again.